JEREMY BIBAUD

HE WHISPERS TORTURED SOUNDS

THE LUNAR WORKSHOP

BOOK ONE

Published by Pequod Publishing.

Publisher's Note: He Whispers Tortured Sounds is a work of fiction. Names, characters, places, and incidents are the product of the author's imagination or are used fictitiously. Any resemblance to actual events, locales, or persons, living or dead, is entirely coincidental.

ISBN (Hardcover): 978-1-7781356-5-1

ISBN (Paperback): 978-1-7781356-3-7

ISBN (eBook): 978-1-7781356-4-4

Library and Archives Canada Cataloguing in Publication data available upon request to the publisher.

For my dad,
who knew Nicholas long before I did.

CHAPTER ONE

THERE ARE eleven ways to break a thing.

Nicholas's thoughts sat heavy in the cradle of his mind. He poked at a yellow, crystalline ornament hanging from a tree as he tried to think of a twelfth way. He tapped the amber bauble again; it swung with unexpected momentum as its string tangled and untangled, sending prismatic spots twirling around the room.

The surrounding walls appeared to shift, moved by shadows created by the slow flames of candles resting throughout the tree. Their glow lit the foil and glass of ornaments, casting him in flickering hues. He sifted the light between his fingers, admiring the change in tone, a trick he only recently discovered. The world was once again aware of his presence.

The sweet scent of cooking meat broke his trance. He teetered through a generous pile of gifts at the foot of the tree, the red and green and gold wrapping paper crinkling against his legs, before reaching the entryway, as he had many times.

"Grandpa?" a child called from beyond the room, still unseen. A small boy bounced in, his bare feet smacking against the wooden floorboards. "Grandpa!" the boy shouted, running straight for an elderly man napping in the corner.

The boy passed through Nicholas like a whisper, barely heard and never felt, before jumping into his grandfather's lap. The old man jolted awake, a look of confusion, then warmth, spread across his wrinkled face.

Nicholas always started at this moment. He did not know the boy or the grandfather. He did not know the house but felt compelled to begin here again and again.

A knock at the door filled the boy with primal energy, excitement discharging through every nerve, followed by the jingling of bells and an eruption of welcoming voices. The vitality, the purity, were both so foreign to Nicholas now. He moved closer to the boy, desperate for any of it.

He told himself the suffering of others shouldn't be observed without some emotional investment, so he freed himself from the moment. If he was being honest with himself, agony is only ever tiresome when not involved. Nicholas returned to the corners, the cracks, the spaces between, the shifting shadows shaped by light he never truly saw, never truly felt.

CHAPTER TWO

Ned Ludd gripped the hilt of his sword. The corner of his mouth twitched. He patted his horse's neck and brushed a few snowflakes from its mane, as much to ease himself as the animal.

A prolonged silence brought on nervous energy. Only moments earlier, the cool evening air sparked with the sounds of colliding metal and stone. The possibility of a trap crept into his bones along with the chill sweeping across the white fields below him.

Ned leaned into his horse and wondered aloud, "If they're caught, how long do you think it would take for those weavers and potters to break under pressure and lead the government soldiers right to me, Whistlejacket?"

His mount shivered and stamped from side to side, bringing up small tufts of snow from under hoof in the same way she did beach foam only a month earlier. Their raids were more frequent as his small army's confidence grew in equal measure to the ink spilled about them by Britain's papers.

The factory here was one of brick, a splash of muted red against the flat, dark palette of the hilly surroundings which, in the low light, lacked all dimension. The group could only do minor damage to the building's exterior, but that did not matter. They were after the machines.

A twig cracked and Ned's eyes darted to the dark collection of bone-thin Scots pine growing behind him, their needled branches reaching outward. He scanned the forest—nothing but displaced shadows moved about by gloom and imagination. A lone tree near the edge of the woodland caught his eye. It stood, like him, overlooking the hills below. Several stars, hanging low in the sky, lit its edges from behind, spreading silver across its trunk. His mind slipped into a distant place. He thought he remembered something, but it remained a whisper, as usual, never materializing into memory.

As if conjured by Ned's will, one of his soldiers sprang from a door on the southern side of the factory and whistled to a horse. The sound, two notes sharp and trained, pierced the distance between him and its source.

Ned shook the snow from his black cloak and pulled his three-cornered hat from his head, dusting off the build-up in its folds before replacing it.

Within a minute, the rider reached him and dismounted.

"General," a soft voice mocked. The soldier curtseyed with exaggeration.

Ned shook his head. "Soldiers don't curtsey, Emma."

"Soldiers don't do a lot of the things I do."

"Why did you leave?"

"The group requested your presence." She smirked.

"I don't join them on raids."

"Yes, sir. The—"

"There's no one else around. You don't need to call me sir, or general."

"Shall I use your real name too?"

"Emma," Ned sighed.

"Give me some credit for trying to maintain an illusion of respect, will you? You never know who is listening."

"You're right. Wait, illusion?"

"Well, you're no general, Ned."

"And this is no army."

"Tell them that," she said, raising a finger toward the factory.

"Why do they want me?"

"They found something."

"What is it?"

"They want you to see it with your own eyes," she said, climbing back onto her horse.

"Did you see it?"

"Yes."

"Shite, just tell me what it is."

Whistlejacket bristled under his exasperation.

"I could tell you, but I would rather you see it with your own eyes too." She winked and pulled her horse around to face the factory. "Come on. Don't pout, my love. Your army awaits."

CHAPTER THREE

"Pick yer feet up, Nicholas." His father's voice split the early morning air with ease.

Nicholas dragged his heels along the stony path to Edinburgh, the sound of rocks scraping underfoot an obnoxious contrast to the stillness of the morning.

"I'm tired." Nicholas took a deep breath, which harboured an even deeper yawn. His slight frame swayed back and forth while he marched.

He trudged along in the enormous shadow of his father, the man's arms wafting the odour of their trade towards Nicholas with every swing. The coal from the mine stuck in every pore, stained every hair. Their clothes were redolent with traces of burnt wood. Before she passed, Nicholas and his younger sister used to squirm into their father's arms after dinner, falling asleep with the heavy scent filling their lungs.

Nicholas drifted to the path's edge, where dark blades of grass still grew and could mask his lazy footfalls, allowing him to shuffle again. He wiped the sleep from his eyes with the brown twill sleeve of his coat, the same scent now attached itself to him. At first, he'd found the odour sharp, and his eyes stung every time he rubbed them with his filthy hands. The smell was imperceptible now, and coal as common to him as any stone, but he couldn't ignore how everything around it lost colour, as if it locked the light inside itself.

"Can you carry me?" Nicholas looked at his father to perk himself up. The glint from a far-off lantern reflected in the old man's eyes.

His father's heavy hand wrapped around his shoulder, bringing him in closer, back onto the rocks, betraying his steps. He picked up the pace again, forgetting the question.

Nicholas stared at the few lingering stars that were not chased away by the coming light. He searched after constellations undiscovered, but found none. He craned his neck so he saw nothing but the waning night sky, and he felt he was no longer under it, but flying above it, looking down at a waking world.

CHAPTER FOUR

EMMA NUDGED her horse back along the trail of dark impressions she'd left in the rising powder. Ned followed. The moonlight afforded them enough light to ride at a brisk pace across the silver field. Emma rode with a confidence Ned lacked. He wasn't comfortable on horses. Emma glanced back at him over her shoulder. From behind, with her dark hair pulled up and the light dim, he might have confused her for one of the young men. Her stiff clothing did not betray the illusion, either. Even at a gallop, the blackened leather held rigid, but the silver buckles around her waist, thighs, and ankles clinked with an increased pitch in the open air.

The cotton factory's red brick exterior paled in the moonlight, as all things did, but Ned guessed it would look no different at midday. As they approached, he noted all but two of the main windows were smashed. Windows were large, expensive for factory owners to replace.

The pair slowed their horses and left them a short distance away.

"You're letting them get lazy," Ned said, motioning to the two intact windows.

She picked up two small rocks and pitched them at the windows. They sailed through the panes, each one taking a small fraction of the entire pane with it.

"Will that do, General?"

He laughed. "Aye. That'll do."

Emma opened the door and held it for Ned. He ducked under the low frame as he entered. He blinked a few times as his eyes searched for something to focus on in the dark.

"Give us some light," Emma called out.

Two sparks burst from the factory floor, and two torches lit up moments later.

A group of bedraggled men and women huddled together inside a ring of bent and broken looms, the very machines that took the livelihoods of several of the women standing here.

Ned entered the circle with his hands behind his back, face stern. It was an unnatural pose and expression he took on in recent months to lend himself more authority.

They stood at attention, their posture not quite up to the standard of an actual regiment of soldiers, but it would suffice.

Ned took a torch and waved it in front of the few individuals closest to him.

"How do ye feel?"

No one responded.

"I said, how do ye feel?"

"Good, sir," one woman in the back, Sarah, ventured.

"Good? Is that why I plucked the lot o' ye from starvation and put a sword in your hands? To feel good?" He kicked one of the bent metal looms; its string and bobbins rattled loose. "Is that why you destroy these machines that took yer very lives from you?"

"Great, sir. I-I feel great," Sarah said.

"Come here," Ned said, motioning with his hand.

Sarah approached and he placed his hands on her shoulders

and spun her to face the rest of the group. He picked up one of the Great Enochs, the massive sledgehammers they wielded, and leaned in close to her ear. "Sarah, lass, tell me, how do you feel when ye raise this hammer above yer sweatin' brow, wi' the blood o' yer ancestors pumping through yer chest?" Ned reached around her with one arm and drummed his fist against her chest in a dull rhythm that stretched out large in the space. "How do you feel when ye let the weight of this world press down on the head of that hammer and you swing, you swing with the cosmic might o' God behind you? How do ye feel, lass?"

She whispered something in response, and a few of the men closest to her laughed.

"Say it again so the wolves outside can hear you."

"Aw, I feel feckin' great, sir," Sarah said.

"Say it again!"

"I feel feckin' great, sir!"

"All o'ye, how do you feel?"

"Feckin' great, sir!" Twenty voices shouted to the moonlit clouds as witness.

"That's better!" Ned roared back at them, before waiting for the group to settle. "Now, what did ye ask me here for? It appears you do not need my help," he said, nodding to the small piles of destruction around them.

"No, sir. We found somethin' you may be interested in seein', sir," Sarah said, emboldened by her proclamation.

"We thought you'd want to see your first reward poster," Emma said.

"A poster?" Ned's curiosity piqued.

She reached into a satchel around her hip and produced a roll of paper.

"Ye had it with you the whole time?" he asked.

"They made me promise not to show you," she said, her smirk not going unnoticed.

A few of the group laughed.

Emma unfurled the yellowed paper and positioned it in the light. The group could no longer contain themselves and burst into fits of laughter.

General Ned Ludd was depicted as a giant wearing a black bonnet with a blue dress and a pink scarf, a shoe on only one foot, and stockings that drooped around his ankles. It read, *Leader of the Luddites.*

He paused, studying the image. "I don't have a beard," Ned said.

"You also don't wear ladies' undergarments over your clothes, Ned," Emma offered.

"Nor under, but this is what I get for leading a band o' out-of-work seamstresses. Thank you all for this… gift." He folded the paper and slid it into his pocket. "Laugh all you want. Let it out. You sorry lot earned it. This is good news. The press has always viewed our raids as nothing more than random strikes by disgruntled workers. This is proof. They now understand that we are coordinated, we are angry, and we will fight to ensure these machines will not replace us. It's an added fortune that our little fiction in creating a leader for our movement is paying off." Ned climbed on the remnants of one of the looms and spread his arms. "I, General Ned Ludd, am now flesh and blood."

The group cheered, their voices booming in the empty factory.

"This will keep the attention off the lot o' you," Ned said.

"And onto you, General," Emma warned.

"If they're looking for a man in women's clothing, I should be safe for some time."

"Yes, but now they have a target. Real or imagined, they'll be looking for you. We should return to the island. Let the stories cool over winter."

"Aye. Good suggestion. We'll get back to the island soon enough. First, let's say we add to my legend. Let's leave another letter for the owner of this now-fine establishment, shall we?"

Emma pulled out a second sheet of paper and handed it to Ned as they all made their way to their horses. He shut the door behind him, and with the butt of his sword against a nail, drove their usual written threat into the blackened oak. He made a slight amendment to his signature before whistling to his horse.

> *Sir, your name is down amongst the darkest hearts. This is to advise you, and the likes of you, to make your wills. Ye have been the darkest enemies of the People on all occasions, Ye have not yet done as ye ought.*
>
> *In truth (and a bonnet),*
>
> *General Ned Ludd*

CHAPTER FIVE

"Yrrebwarts!" Nicholas said.

His father grunted. "It's too early for games."

"Please," he said, stretching the word out as long as he could. "Yrrebwarts." He tugged on a loose thread hanging from around a button on his coat.

His father remained silent. The only sound that passed between them was their metronomic footsteps. Nicholas sighed.

His father relented. "Strawberry."

"Aye!" Nicholas laughed. "Now I have a hard one. Dnaltocs—"

"Scotland."

"Wait, I wasn't finished! Dnaltocs si ym reverof emoh."

"Scotland is my forever home."

"Aye. Your turn." Nicholas skipped ahead a few paces, youthful energy burning through him now.

"Tub serusaelp era ekil seippop daerps." The words fell from his lips like a chant.

Nicholas whispered to himself while he sorted the words in his head. "Mmm, something about poppies?"

"Aye, but pleasures are like poppies spread." His father continued, "Uoy ezies eht rewolf, sti moolb si dehs."

"I don't know. Too many words."

"You seize the flower; its bloom is shed. Ro ekil eht wons sllaf ni eht revir."

Nicholas's face lit up with realization. "Like the snow falls in the river?"

"A tnemom etihw, neht stlem reverof."

"A moment white, then melts forever."

His father grunted approval.

"You always do Burns," Nicholas said.

"Aye. Not a finer wordsmith. Shouldn't we know him front and back?

"I like to write my own."

His father laughed. "That is good too. Yrrebwarts was funnier than mine."

"I think so too." Nicholas snorted. "Yrrebwarts. That's the best backwards word so far."

Edinburgh grew closer with every step. The castle, visible for miles, still cast the city in enormous shadow, the morning light threatening to throw it off as a blanket.

"Nico!" A delicate voice broke the dim mood created by the looming capital. His friend Samantha sat on top of a boulder near the path.

"Sam! What are you doing?"

"I'm going to the city too! Working. Like you." She smiled at him, tucking her red hair beneath her blue bonnet. Several loose strands still hung down over her eyes. Sliding off the rock, she balanced a lantern on her descent. A warm, amber glow poured over her, corralling shadows to the wrinkles and folds of her faded green dress. She approached, spinning the moist stem of a thistle between her fingers, needles pressing into the skin of her thumb and index finger.

"Look!" she said, with far more excitement than either Nicholas or his father could have mustered at this hour. She tossed the thistle and raised her wrist to the light, displaying a small turquoise stone suspended from a black leather bracelet.

"That's lovely, Sam. Is it new?" Nicholas's father asked.

"It was my ma's. It is my ma's. And it was her ma's, but she let me wear it today."

The stone featured a small carving of a sprig of holly. Sam ran the tip of her finger across the grooves.

"Keep it safe. Edinburgh is full of thieves," said Nicholas's father.

"I will." Sam covered it with her other hand.

"Where are you working?" Nicholas asked as Sam joined them on the path, leaving the lantern on a fencepost.

"I don't know what it is yet, but I get to wear a dress, and this is my only one and it's beautiful."

Even in the reduced light, Nicholas knew she was beaming, smoothing the wrinkles from her dress as they walked. "Dresses are stupid," he said.

His father smacked the back of his head.

"Sorry, it's good, I guess."

"You're jealous because you can't wear them."

"No," he said, the best retort he could muster in the moment. "Better hope you aren't blacking. On a hot day, the stink of feet will choke a rat!" Nicholas managed a small laugh.

Sam laughed back.

"How's your pa? I haven't seen him in a fortnight," Nicholas's father asked.

"He's taking care of Mum."

"Stay close to us until we get to the city, then. Your parents would never forgive me if something happened to you. You're being a good lass?"

"I am. Mum's always fussing with the baby when she's feeling up to it. She doesn't notice me much anymore." Sam moved from one side of Nicholas to the other, a sly smile flashing from under her bonnet.

"Babies are a lot of work. I'm sure she notices you."

"Aye, you're too loud not to notice!" Nicholas nudged Sam and ran ahead a few steps.

"Don't make me hurt you in front of your pa, Nicholas Locherbie," Sam tugged on the sleeves of her dress, composing herself.

"Try it! You can't hurt me, Sam." Nicholas walked backwards in front of her, his arms stretched open wide, waiting for her to make a move.

"I could most definitely hurt you. I've hurt many boys bigger than you," she said, affecting her speech with a maturity she often invoked when trying to prove a point.

His father laughed. "Careful, lad."

"Thank you, Mr. Locherbie," she said. "It's nice to know there are men who still respect a lady."

Nicholas scrunched his face. "Lady? We were digging warty toads out of the river last week." He turned forward again, falling back in line beside his friend, who now walked with her arms crossed, her gaze turned from Nicholas.

They were quiet for the rest of their trek. The sun crested over Arthur's Seat, the massive hill to the east, pushing the remnants of night into the nooks and closes of the city. Edinburgh Castle stood within a fiery halo burning at its edges, changing the mood but not the castle's dominance of the skyline.

The trio approached a split in the road where mineworkers mustered to wait for the wagons that would shuttle them to the mine. Nicholas couldn't remember the last time he'd walked past this point into the city.

"See you tomorrow," Sam murmured. She broke away and continued toward Morrison Street.

"You should be nicer to her, Nicholas. Her ma hasn't been right since the baby."

"She should be nicer to me too!"

"I'm not Sam's father. I'm yours. Be nice to her. She is a good lass. You'll always have time to make new enemies, but not enough to make new friends," his father said, trailing off as they reached their destination.

Nicholas rolled his eyes, a mannerism he learned from Sam.

"Do you understand me?"

"Aye."

Ahead, the muster point filled with the ragged, weary army of men who worked the mine. Their gaunt faces and dark eyes gave them the countenance of a host of pub brawl losers.

Nicholas and his father joined their ranks.

CHAPTER SIX

A STORM ROLLED across the Shetland Islands as the sun slid below the horizon, the jewel-green hills turned black by dark clouds. A light rain dotted the animal skins laid across the cylindrical opening of the Broch of Mousa. The towering structure on the edge of the island, ancient and weathered, was a cool, dry space. Inside, Ned sat up in his bed, massaging tight muscles around his knees.

"You rub any higher up your leg and you will not need me tonight," Emma said. She glanced at Ned's reflection in the mirror while she applied a deep red colour to her lips.

"It's the weather. My legs ache when it turns bitter. Just warming them."

"I thought that's what I was here for," she said, before pulling a wide-toothed comb that looked more like the jaw of a wild animal through her hair. The outline of her pale legs and backside peeked through the muslin. She bent over at a steep angle to use the small mirror. The dim light from a candle placed on the vanity lit up the right side of her body. The paisley embroidering sewn into the delicate fabric did little to hide the details.

Ned continued to knead the knots from his legs; the motion didn't provide much relief, but it felt good.

"How do you feel about sharing a bed with a man who has the aches of someone three times your age?"

"I've shared the bed of men who really were three times my age, Ned. You at least don't come with the wrinkles and the spots." She ran her thumb across a brush. The candlelight caught bits of powder as they puffed upward from the bristles and fell to the dirt below. "Besides, you don't know how old you are, anyway. Maybe you are just an old pervert."

He laughed. "You still believe me? Even after all this time?"

"I do. It seems an odd thing to lie about not remembering your childhood, and I can't think of any real benefit for doing so."

Ned pushed the broadside of his hands into the flesh of his leg. "Sometimes when I'm alone, I feel cool ocean air wash over me in the middle of a dry field or I'll hear the bustle of a market in the stillness of a cave. I can't help but think it's memories coming unstuck inside me. Nothing ever comes of it, though." He glanced at Emma to gauge her reaction, but she gave him nothing. "I would tell you more if I could."

"I know. You cannot remember your youth and I wish I could forget mine. I made my peace with it."

"I would gladly trade afflictions."

"Be careful what you wish for, old man."

"Not for me, for you."

"You need not say such sweet things, Ned. I've already decided I'm sleeping with you tonight."

Ned laughed. "Do I have a say?"

"Do you want one?" she asked, watching him in the mirror. "Ned, I only care for who you are, not who you were. If it takes a man to forget his childhood to turn out as fine as you, then I wish this malady on all men."

"Who's being sweet now?"

A North Sea breeze found its way through the thick stone-stacked wall and Ned pulled the blankets tighter around him. Despite the constant rain, the near inexhaustible supply of candles and animal furs kept them warm. An army of tradesmen at your side made it much easier to live on a remote island.

Finishing in the mirror, Emma turned, a candle flickering in her hands. Her black hair settled along her collar bones. Golden shadows played against her smooth, white skin as the flame shifted in front of her. Her gown ran the length of her body. The smooth cotton rose from the earthen floor to the bottom of her breasts, leaving them exposed to the midnight air.

"Do you like it?" she asked.

"I've seen nothing like it."

"That's not what I asked."

"Aye, I like it."

"Good. I asked one of the women to make it for me. She gave it to me as a gift."

"You shouldn't take gifts from them, Emma. They have so little."

"She refused when I tried to pay her the first time and was insulted the second time. And you don't seem to mind living in the broch while they all sleep outside in tents."

She placed the candle on a small wooden table beside the bed and swung a leg over Ned, positioning herself on top of him. She leaned over and blew out the candle, her golden glow replaced with a bluish hue as the darkness raced in. Ned gripped her waist, his thumbs pressed into her hips. Even through the gown, the smooth scars that intersected the muscles of her stomach rubbed against his hands. They were all over her body, her legs, arms, back. She squeezed his fingers into her chest as she ground her body into his lap.

Emma slid her hand behind his head, pulling it toward her. Her hair fell into his face, mingling with his mouth as he pressed his lips into the warm, moist space between her breasts. He breathed in, smelled the earth and rain mix with her scent. She gripped a fistful of his hair and pulled his head back to meet his eyes.

"Can I call you by your real name tonight? Please, General?"

Ned laughed. "Permission granted."

"James," she said with an exaggerated moan before continuing, "Locherbie." She smiled down at him and giggled, her body still writhing against his. "It always feels so wrong."

He relaxed into her; his muscles released. Even the pain in his legs dulled.

"Where are my hands, James?" she whispered.

Even in the dark, Ned was certain she could see the confusion on his face.

"Where are my hands, General?"

"I… one of them is on the back of my head," he whispered back.

"And the other?"

He paused for a few moments. "I don't know."

She brought her head down to his shoulder, her mouth against his ear. "This is when I would have killed you."

He exhaled in frustration, pushing Emma off his lap.

"Emma, you don't need to do this. You don't need to prepare me for the possibility of death at every moment."

"I don't want to prepare you, Ned. I want you to prepare yourself. And you don't. Still."

He sat up and slid his feet from under the blankets to the cold floor.

"I shouldn't have to protect myself from you. And I hope I won't be in bed with a government soldier when they come to arrest me. When the time comes, I'll be ready."

"They aren't coming to arrest you. They're coming to hang you. You do not know how they'll find you, but they will."

"Can we not go one evening without thinking of my death?"

She pressed her body against his back and wrapped her legs around his midsection, her feet crossing over his lap. Her warm cheek rested against him. "I am sorry, my love," she paused. For a moment, it appeared she might relent, "But no. You're a wanted man now."

She kissed his back and ran her fingers through his wavy hair, massaging his scalp. "Come back to me, James. We can still enjoy the rest of the night." She pulled one of his arms back, slid his hand under her gown, and pressed it to the warmth between her legs.

CHAPTER SEVEN

On a foggy morning like this one, the bruised waters of the Firth of Forth were infinite. The mist lost all depth when it rolled in this low and, to Nicholas, who wanted nothing more than to run into the waves, appeared flat, like a wall. It made him claustrophobic, as if Scotland itself was squeezing him in.

The water, for all its menace, kept a slow pace with the wagon. Nicholas, his father, and the men with them jumped from it before it came to a stop and scrambled off the soggy path toward the mine.

They were late to arrive, as they often were, but they did so without notice and melted into the long lines marching into the dark tunnels. Nicholas felt the cold from the morning's ride already giving way to the heat circulating from the many bodies around him. Lanterns cast their skin in a familiar amber glow. His father grabbed a pick and a shovel from a pile of tools near the entrance and handed them both to him.

They walked in silence for several minutes before reaching the exact spot they'd left the day before. The sounds of metal crashing against rock rippled through the tunnels. It was loud at first, then dulled through repetition.

Nicholas's father used the pick to cut away at the coal while Nicholas shovelled the dark rock into a nearby cart. He was an anomaly compared to the other children, already seven years old with less than a year of experience.

After only a few months on the job, Nicholas ached to be back at home, wandering the forests around their hamlet, chasing Sam down to the river. He missed the sun and the water and the colour. On the best days, he would turn his mind off and allow those twelve hours to slip away until he found himself on the wagon heading back to Edinburgh. Today would not be one of those days, each of his father's strikes a punctuation marking only a few seconds. He counted the number of strikes in one minute, and then in one hour, before trying to determine how many strikes his father needed to reach before they could leave.

The sound of knocking wood interrupted his counting. The shift manager, Mr. Steward, ambled up the tunnel, striking the shaft of his shovel against those of each miner he passed. He stopped at Nicholas.

"Locherbie, we need Nicholas," he shouted above the clanging.

His father stopped, out of breath, "Again? You used him last week."

"And we'll use him as many times as we need to. He ain't your son in this mine. He's a hired hand. Unless you don't want him to be."

"John, please. Let him stay."

Mr. Steward's face softened. "You know I don't like it, but your boy has already seen the new tunnels and none of the other bairns have shown up. I'll make sure he minds the door since he drammed last week." He leaned in closer to Nicholas's father and said in a hushed tone, "James, I'm sending my son in too. We need the children opening the gates to get the coal out and let some good air in. The men will suffocate down there."

Go with him.

A voice, clear as a bell on a Highland night, rang inside Nicholas's mind. He looked up at his father and Mr. Steward as they argued. It wasn't either of them. There was no one else around.

Prove yourself.

Again, the words entered his skull, compelling him. He found himself speaking, the words already leaving his lips before he knew it. "I'll go. I'll do it," he said.

Mr. Steward put his hand on Nicholas's shoulder, but he wriggled away from him.

His father sighed before kneeling and straightening the boy's coat collar. "Be good for Mr. Steward, you hear? Listen to every word he tells you." His father's eyes caught his own. "Look at me," his father said, commanding his attention. "I love you, Nicholas."

He handed his shovel back to his father and turned to face Mr. Steward.

"Yrrebwarts," his father whispered behind him.

Nicholas laughed. He wanted to look back at his father, but he kept thinking about what Mr. Steward said. He was a hired hand here, not his father's son.

CHAPTER EIGHT

WHAT SHOULD HAVE BEEN a lazy morning in their bed, the air thick with salt, the embers of a night together stoked at their waking, was instead interrupted by frantic clanging on the metal door of the broch.

Ned snapped to and reached for his sword. It wasn't there.

"Here," Emma said, already dressed and extending his blade to him.

"What are they on about? And why didn't you wake me? Where are my breeches?"

"I do not know, Ja—Ned," she said, catching herself. "But you can find your own clothes," she said, dropping his sword onto the bed.

Ned found his trousers bunched up under the bed and pulled them on. He grabbed his weapon and marched towards the gate. The source of the din was a large man with a beard, red in the face, his name beyond Ned's grasp. Sinclair, maybe?

"Sir, a ship approaches!"

Ned froze. "A ship? Here?"

"Aye, sir. Sorry, sir. Not a government boat. A private hire. Small crew."

"Thank you for waking me, Sinclair."

"'Tis Stuart, sir."

"Stuart, my apologies. I'll join you. Emma!"

"You need not shout, Ned." She placed her hand on his bare chest. "I'm here. Breathe. Get dressed. I'll go out before you."

Ned nodded and did as she instructed. He breathed in through his nose, out through his mouth, like she showed him. The breathing helped centre him, calm his anxiety. He pulled his shirt over his head and readied himself in the mirror.

He wiped a few beads of sweat from his forehead with his index finger. Serving as a general felt more like acting than being. Real or not, a panicked general could not instil confidence.

These people followed him because he differed from them, and he knew this. And he knew how to maintain it. He slept apart from them and did not join them in raids or celebrations. This distance, and the mystery surrounding his past, was enough to give him near-mythical status. They whispered about him, but he gave them no answers. In part because he had none.

He wrapped a belt around his waist, his sword along with it.

The wanted poster they'd found stuck out from the pocket of his coat, punctuating the moment. There was a small twinge in his chest. The Shetland Islands kept them safe from Scottish law, but was close enough to wage sweeping attacks across the mainland factories throughout the warmer months. It also kept them isolated from the larger rebellion laying waste to factories across Britain, where authorities killed or hanged the Luddites, as they were now called. The news shook his army, but their continued success and safety soon pushed the fear from them and solidified his place as their leader. It did nothing to help his conscience, though.

Emma reminded him these events were happening long before he arrived and, for all he knew, other men had also taken up the name of Ned Ludd to divert attention. He wasn't to blame for their deaths. The words comforted him then, but their warmth wore off soon after. They invented Ned Ludd as a device to keep the authorities chasing a single leader rather than focusing on the mob. It didn't always work, though.

He placed his three-cornered hat atop his head.

"Ned?" Emma called to him.

He walked with her to the edge of a rise and spied the approaching vessel. His small army, standing in a loose formation, stared on, many of them with their hands resting on the hilts of their swords. They hadn't seen a ship approach the Isle of Mousa since they arrived.

Ned called the group together. They shuffled over to him, some unwilling to take their eyes off the water. It gave him time to survey them. He had to admit, they possessed a particular flair, many of them draped in ridiculous fabrics and bright colours, a product of their crafts. Their ostentatiousness gave the entire effort a swagger that emboldened them. It kept them from becoming idle, at any rate.

"You're scared. I see that. You need not be. They aren't flying a government flag. For all we know, it's a bunch of lost fishermen. I'll take some of you to meet them. The rest will stay here. If something should go wrong, you have your hammers and you have your swords."

One of the women stepped forward. "Sir, we've never attacked people."

"I don't believe you're going to have to, at least not today. But if it should come to it, do not hesitate. They've taken your livelihood, don't let them take your life."

He motioned to Emma and two of the men to follow him down the path.

"You're quite convincing when you need to be," she whispered to him.

"Aye, the coat helps. You can barely see me sweating through my clothes."

She laughed. "It'll get easier."

A small dinghy carrying two men coursed through the water. One rowed, the other stood.

They reached the water as the boat hit the shore. The one standing leapt from it into the ankle-deep water. He was older, distinguished. He ran his hand against his damp forehead and pushed a few white curls into place before advancing up the beach.

Ned's soldiers took a step forward, forming a small spearhead in front of him.

The man stopped, startled. "Greetings, may I ask whose beach I have arrived at?"

His expression was warm, familiar even.

Emma addressed him, "You've reached the Broch of Mousa. It's closed to visitors. Return to your ship and move along to the next island."

The man's face grew long with disappointment. "That's a shame," he said as he reached into his coat.

Emma drew her sword. The tip stopped only a foot away from his throat.

"Wait! I'm merely reaching for a letter."

"For who?" said Emma.

"For me. The letter came to me. It instructed me to come here."

Emma motioned for him to hand it to her. He did, stretching his arm out under the steady blade. She flipped open the soggy paper and read it to herself before passing it back.

Ned pushed through the bodies in front of him, relaxing them as he did. He read it for himself. It was an invitation to the island. Stranger still, it was in Ned's own handwriting.

"I didn't send this," he whispered to Emma.

"It's your writing."

"I know, but I didn't send this."

Ned and Emma broke their huddle and addressed the man again. "Who are you?" Ned asked.

The man's face softened, and he smiled before bowing forward. "My name is James Locherbie."

CHAPTER NINE

NICHOLAS BENT and squinted into the tunnel. The light did not penetrate even an inch beyond the opening. Cailean, Mr. Steward's son, disappeared inside, his lantern already absorbed, his feet lost in the dark. Mr. Steward handed Nicholas his own lantern.

"You know how it works, lad. When you reach the first gate, close it behind Cailean. Only open when you hear him coming with a cart. Pull on the rope. It'll open with little effort."

"How long do I stay in there?"

"About another ten hours. Did you bring a lunch?"

Nicholas shook his head. "I forgot it."

"Here, take this." Mr. Steward reached into a pack slung over his shoulder and pulled out a dry roll and small piece of cheese. He gave them to Nicholas.

Without protest, Nicholas stuffed the food into his coat pocket, got down on his hands and knees, and entered the tunnel. He pushed the lamp along the rough ground ahead of him, coughing every so often on the dust it disturbed. The shaft was only a few feet high and the roof uneven. He stayed low and kept his hands close to his body, not wanting to catch them on a sharp edge.

After several minutes of slow progress, his light revealed the metal door. He leaned against the tunnel wall and stretched his legs out, the space wider here. He hung his light on a wooden hook and it cast across several markings scrawled onto the gate's surface. Most were initials, arranged like scribbled stars orbiting a greater message that read:

SHUT THIS DOOR
THAT MEANS YOU

Nicholas looked back; he saw nothing further than a few feet and not a single sound penetrated the darkness.

After an hour of blind silence, the creak of worn wheels reached him. He leaped up, bumping his head on the rock above. He grunted, but fumbled in the dirt for the rope and, finding it, heaved. The door swung open in time to let Cailean through, but also struck his lantern, sending it careening into the cavern wall. Its flame went out.

Nicholas cursed, but focused on keeping the gate open.

The cart rolled into view from behind Cailean, tied to a rope that ran up between his legs and around his waist. The other boy didn't speak. Nicholas didn't take offence. He drammed a few times already, and it didn't leave you with enough energy for pleasantries. Cailean, his movements heavy and rhythmic, pulled away from Nicholas and out of sight. Without a working light, he groped around the tunnel to find the spot he had sat in earlier. Broken glass crunched beneath his feet. He removed his coat and laid it on the ground under him.

In the quiet, his own breathing annoyed him. After that, his heartbeat, followed by a raging current, the blood flowing through his head. Moving around, making some noise was important to distract himself. Something skittered from one of his jacket pockets. He searched for his lunch and discovered the cheese missing. Only the roll remained. Defeated, he took a bite. The stale bread hurt his jaw to chew, but the sound of laboured chewing provided a welcome respite from hearing his own internal workings.

Cailean returned. The boy startled when he came upon Nicholas, having not seen any light. He raised his own lantern and saw the broken one beside the door. He sighed and muttered something. Nicholas pulled the ventilation gate open again. Cailean passed and the impenetrable quiet again surrounded him.

Nicholas found a small rock next to his foot and tossed it up, trying to catch it in the dark. It thudded into the dirt with every miss until, finally, he caught it. The stone slapped against the pad of his hand. He caught it three more times in a row. He tried for a fifth consecutive catch, a world record, no doubt. It fell into his hand at the same moment a loud crack, crunch, and a rumble echoed nearby. He moved closer to the gate before a tremor shook the barrier from the other side.

The noise grew, then a flurry of pounding caused him to jerk his head away. He scrambled to the dirt and found the rope, gripped it tight and yanked, throwing himself back at the same time.

Cailean burst through, his lantern flooding the shaft just in time for Nicholas to see the roof of the tunnel collapse. The ceiling split in half and the rock above crushed the boy, the light extinguished at the same time.

Then the supports above Nicholas failed and the sound of bending metal sent him into a panic. A thick cloud of dust clogged his throat as he clambered on his hands and knees back up the tunnel.

He cut his arms and legs, scraped his head against the shifting rock. His body was numb, but he moved on instinct. Then the chaos stopped. Everything fell quiet. The blood rushing through his ears returned, dust settled on the back of his head. A strange sensation grew in his legs, as if they were somehow far away from them, like he crawled to this point without his lower half. He tried to lift his head and something inside him cracked. The pain eclipsed the adrenaline, and he screamed and cried into the stones, his own anguish joining a chorus of others, so close they echoed inside of him, bouncing off the crumbling rock. They fell away eventually, reduced to whispers. Then he heard his father's name above them.

James.

The name was distant and loud. His father's name. He heard it so infrequently it stuck with him as he faded. His father's name. His father's name.

CHAPTER TEN

"YOUR NAME IS JAMES LOCHERBIE?" Emma asked, her sword arm unwavering.

"Aye."

"Have we met?" Ned asked, resting his hand on Emma's arm, encouraging her to lower her weapon. She did.

James nodded. "I do not believe so. I'm sure I would have remembered," he paused, "her, at the very least."

Emma sheathed her sword. "A stranger sends you a letter, and you set sail for an isolated island? That seems unwise. Unbelievable, even."

"I had reason to believe I'd find my son here."

"Your son?" Ned responded.

"Aye, I lost him as a young lad. I've been looking for him ever since. When I got this letter I thought, hoped, it was from him."

"A bit of a leap to assume that, no?"

"Perhaps, but for someone who believes things happen for a reason, not as far as you might think. The penmanship is like my own."

"Send your ship away," Emma said.

James turned, but hesitated.

"Send your ship away or you may leave with it."

He waved to the man in the small boat, who rowed back to the ship.

Ned stepped forward. "I am General Ned Ludd. I didn't send you this letter, but this is my handwriting."

James's mouth fell open. "I knew it. I knew it the moment I saw you. You look like—" his breath caught in his throat and his eyes welled up. He moved towards Ned, but Emma stepped between them.

"I'm sorry. I've heard your name. You must have many enemies," James stammered, composing himself.

"Many," Emma replied.

"You'll have to forgive our lack of hospitality. I'm not even sure where to begin. If what you say is true," he let the sentence hang between them. "Let's get off this beach before the fog rolls in. We'll take you back to our camp. You can answer a few questions along the way," Ned said.

He strained to remain composed. The man standing in front of him might hold the answer to every question he ever asked himself.

Emma slid her arm under his and pulled close. "Easy, Ned."

She was right. Too many people depended on him to allow for a distraction like this, but he couldn't shake the familiarity of his face. The truth was only a single body away.

CHAPTER ELEVEN

Emma's stomach clenched. This man's sudden appearance just circumvented all the time she spent preparing Ned for some awful, unseen event. She hoped for some obvious sign that he wasn't who he claimed, but she admitted, to herself, he looked the part.

Walking between them, she didn't know if she was shielding Ned from an attack or shielding James from Ned's eagerness. Ned's eyes hadn't betrayed his thoughts like this since they first met.

–

Emma hadn't eaten in two days. Her head ached and her legs weakened, trudging through the muddy streets of Dundee. With every other step, deepening puddles threatened to remove her boots, but she refused to stop following her mark.

They were a strange lot; their dress was unlike anything she'd seen. Unusual cuts, bright colours, although dulled by travel, still caught her eye. They were buying supplies for a long journey. One of them, a handsome man who wore a three-cornered hat and lacked the eccentricity of his companions, paid for everything from a small, red sack on his belt. She waited in the shadows of eaves and around the stone corners of pubs and kirks for the lot to leave the city. They travelled with two large wagons and several children. That is, slow.

Setting off north as the sun set, the group clearly wasn't waiting until morning. This suited Emma for several reasons, all of which related to making theft easier. First, a horse.

She followed the small caravan out of town before breaking from the road towards a nearby stable. As she approached, she spied a young man with a round face equal to his belly, brushing a tawny horse, its mane a braid of intricate knots. Emma pulled an empty wine bottle from her bag and stumbled from the trees into the light, acting drunk and in need of a big, strong man to help her find her way.

She giggled and took a swig from the empty bottle before falling to her knees in a splash of her own dress.

"Lass? Are you okay?" The stable hand rushed to help. As he stooped down, Emma rose and rang the bottle off the side of his head. The man went limp and fell forward, his face kissing the dirt before the rest of him followed.

She hurried to the horse. "Aren't you beautiful?" she cooed, coaxing it from the stable. The young man groaned. No time for a saddle. She leaped up and swung her leg over the horse. It protested, so she ran her hand along its thick neck while she whispered soft sounds into its ears. "We don't have time to get friendly, horse." Emma noticed a nameplate above the stall. "Whistlejacket, is it? Work with me and I promise you all the carrots you can eat." She murmured the name a few more times and Whistlejacket settled. Emma nudged the horse towards the caravan. They would both eat well tonight.

The wagons were beyond the light of the city when she caught up. She stayed off the road and put some distance between them and her and followed until the group stopped to make camp.

Relieved, Emma swung herself off Whistlejacket, her thighs aching. "I know you felt that as much as I did, but please don't leave me. I can't tie you up, but if you leave me, no carrots for you, understand?"

Whistlejacket grunted.

Emma tied off her dress to make walking through the brush a little easier. By the time she reached the camp's outskirts, mud covered her legs. The group set up fast and only a pair remained by the fire to keep watch. Neither of them was the man with the coin.

She stalked the perimeter of the camp until she could put the wagons between her and the campfire. With the tree cover no longer necessary, she slinked through the thick grass before squatting beside a tent separate from the rest. A light snore emanated from inside. She slid back the tent flap; the three-cornered hat lay at her feet. Shrugging, she took it, flipping it over in hopes of using it as a bowl for her plunder. She crept alongside her sleeping mark to a pile of clothes in the opposite corner. Rifling through the garments, her fingers struck velvet. The small bag clinked at her touch. She lifted it into the hat.

As she did, an enormous shadow swept across the surface of the tent. Too large. Her stomach dropped.

Whistlejacket stamped the ground around the tent, drawing the attention of the two men by the fire. Their confused voices rose as they approached the rogue horse.

"Don't move." The man beside her spoke.

She turned to face him. He sat up, his features cast in darkness.

"Who are you?" he asked.

She considered charm, but with a handful of the man's coins, that would be a tough sell. As usual, she went with violence.

Shifting her weight, she sprung on top of him, wrapped her fingers around his neck and pressed on his throat with her thumbs as hard as she could. She surprised him, but she also underestimated him. He struck her across the face with a wild fist, but she did not relent. He underestimated her.

His hands continued swinging even as he tried to roll out from beneath her, and grabbed a fistful of the tent, tearing it open.

The men preoccupied by the excited horse were now in clear view. Their expressions turned from frustration to shock as she wrestled. They ripped the tent from its posts and pulled her off their breathless leader.

She struggled at first, but the men forced her to the ground.

The man she tried to rob caught his breath as he struggled to his feet. "You're not dressed like a government soldier," he coughed. "An assassin would have slit my throat before going for my coin purse." He coughed. "Who are you?"

"I'm someone who would be a lot richer if I had walked." Emma said, staring at her equine traitor.

"Aye, I'm definitely keeping this one. She's a bit o' good luck, if you ask me." He reached up alongside the horse, panic in its eyes. He shushed it, coaxing it down until it settled.

"Bring her to the fire," he said to the men.

They lifted Emma to her feet and did as instructed.

Near the cooking pit, orange light flickered across their faces. She recognised him but couldn't place his face.

"What's your name?" he asked.

"Emma," she said.

"Emma? That's all?"

"Emma Breugadaire."

"A strange name for a strange woman."

The commotion roused the rest of the camp and several of the group gathered around.

"Who are you people?" she asked.

"That you don't know is the only reason we haven't tied you to a tree and left you for the wolves."

She studied the faces of the group. Scared mothers held their sons and daughters behind them, fathers white-knuckled shovels and hammers. Their leader's face was soft, unblemished. No signs of battle. Only light reflected in his eyes.

She laughed. "No, I don't think you would do that," she said.

A child, a young girl, carrying a raggedy doll, caught her attention. The doll's loose threads brushed the dirt.

Then it struck her. She knew him, but he made no sign that he knew her. She hoped it would remain that way.

–

Marching alongside Ned now, suspicion growing inside her, she renewed her vow to never leave his side. Not again.

CHAPTER TWELVE

It could be dangerous for Ned to believe the stranger, but it didn't stop him from noting how their gait matched, how their hair curled the same way, how their eyes were the same deep blue. Their bodies, both built like crates, lumbered off the beach. It was laughable how fast his mind raced for any evidence to support the claim. Then again, why should he be so quick to doubt it? It was more plausible that his father came searching for him than it would be for an assassin or a government agent to use his lost father, a reality very few knew, to trick him. He took Emma's hand and squeezed it as they continued up the shifting sand.

"I don't know where to begin. It's not every day a man steps out of the fog claiming to be your father."

"Do you not remember me at all?"

"The truth is—," Ned started.

"You're asking more questions than answering," Emma finished. "Who was on the ship with you? Where did you sail from?"

"I didn't know the men on the ship. A fishing crew with a

sturdy vessel I found in Edinburgh. I paid them to bring me here," James replied.

"You'd have to pay a fishing ship a lot of coin to convince them to come up this way."

"Don't I know it," James said. "It seems to have been worth the price, though."

Ned interjected, "Let's save the rest of the interrogation for later. James, you claim to be my father, but I have no way of knowing if what you say is true."

James stepped out in front of him. "Do you not see it? We look identical," James said, exasperated.

Ned looked to Emma for confirmation. She sighed and then nodded. "The eyes, nose, mouth. It is uncanny."

The trio continued towards the camp. The Luddites murmured to one another, peeking from their tents and from around corners, watching their visitor with unease.

"Everyone, this is James Locherbie. He is our guest—"

"Mm, prisoner," Emma said.

Ned raised an eyebrow at her. She raised one back.

"James is our guest and prisoner. Either way, we treat both with dignity and respect."

A few in the group asked his reason for coming to the island.

"I won't hide his reason for coming from you. He claims to be my father. As you know, I don't remember much of my childhood, including my family. So, I don't take this claim lightly."

A flurry of whispers zipped its way through the crowd.

"When I know more, I will tell you, but there's nothing to fear. He won't be leaving without our blessing."

The Luddites returned to their tents, their fires, other distractions, content with knowing they were not under attack.

Ned led James up the path to the broch. He kept pace, not slowed by age. A light rain slicked the stones of the hulking structure. The gate groaned as they entered, away from the coming storm.

Inside, they wandered the room, feigning interest in the mundane objects scattered about, if only to delay taking a seat.

Emma broke the silence. "Are we going to sit or continue this awkward dance around the room?"

Ned's shoulders fell. "She's right. We need to talk, but it'll be uncomfortable."

"Of course. I want to. I'll answer any questions you have. Uncomfortable or not."

"Who gave you the letter?" Emma asked.

"A strange fellow. A merchant in Edinburgh. Peculiar, but he knew me and where I could find you. It may sound unbelievable, but it's not as if I go about telling everyone I lost my son. He convinced me."

"It still seems hasty," Emma said.

"I don't expect you to understand."

"Help me then."

James sat, Ned and Emma followed.

"I have been searching for my son since he was a child. It has cost me every coin to my name, every relationship I had. I bear the marks of every scrap of information, every lead I choked from anyone who I thought could help me. This time, the information came to me. Call me a fool, but after decades of relentless pursuit, it felt," he looked at Ned, "it felt like a reward."

The room fell quiet for a time.

"I'm going to let the two of you continue, but before I leave, do you have a name for the merchant?"

"Chapman. No address, but he hangs about in the crannies o' Holyrood. He sells oddities. Junk mostly. Just off the Mile. Anyone will be able to point you to him."

Emma pursed her lips. "I'll ask the rest of the camp if they've heard of him. Maybe one of them let something slip the last time we resupplied. We need to learn how he knew we were here. If he knows, others will too. We may need to visit this Chapman, Ned. Sooner than later."

"Aye. I know."

"I'll let the two of you get reacquainted."

The pair let out a nervous chuckle. She shook her head, the tension pushing her from the room. The gate creaked shut behind her.

James spoke first, "So, you're a General?"

"Of a sort," Ned replied with a trace of pride. "What kind of work do you do?"

"Ah, carpentry," James said.

Ned's face lit up. "I make small carvings for the kids here sometimes. It feels like something I've always done, but I can't be sure of that."

James looked puzzled. "Why not?"

Ned stared into the fire.

"I suppose I should let you ask the questions."

Ned nodded.

"Where would you like to start?" James asked.

CHAPTER THIRTEEN

THE RAIN STOPPED, and the fog receded. Mousa returned to its natural greens and blues. Emma closed the gate to the Broch behind her and walked to the top of a low hill. She looked west to the mainland's purple crags. The sea battered the coast, chipping away invisible bits of earth. Her eyes turned south, where dark clouds persisted. Edinburgh. She hadn't been to the capital in years and would be happy to never visit again.

No one here would have leaked their location on any of their supply runs. They had everything at stake. The children might have spoken the name of the island aloud, but even they would never have spoken Ned's real name. She doubted many of them were even aware of it.

Along the path, she encountered two girls splashing in fresh puddles, the fringe of their dresses slick with mud and stained by dark water. Emma surprised them by jumping in. The splash of water rose above their heads. They laughed even as she completely drenched them. Emma asked them the last time they'd been off the island. Months ago.

She continued in this way, interrogating friends and families.

She felt horrid, but needed one of them to reveal something, anything, if only to give her an excuse to avoid travelling to the city. When she reached the final family, she already knew it would lead nowhere. With each denial, the truth of the matter grew stronger in the back of her mind: someone knew they were here, and she had no idea how.

Worse still, they were toying with them by sending this man claiming to be Ned's father. Was it a distraction or a warning?

A thunderclap from the south punctuated her thought. They would leave for Edinburgh in the morning.

CHAPTER FOURTEEN

NICHOLAS WOKE a few minutes before arriving, his head still foggy. The hay gave him insulation and the crates shelter from chilly winds, at least.

"I thought you died back there 'tween the tongues. Would've been a story to tell your pa, wouldn't it?" Mr. Chapman shouted over his shoulder, enunciating every letter.

Nicholas didn't feel like talking yet. His father had arranged the journey with Mr. Chapman. He would bring Nicholas to the mill for work. Something better suited for a boy with a limp.

"The River Clyde, this is. You'll know it well. The whole of New Lanark is built along its edge. The mill, in particular. You'll see."

Nicholas cleared his throat before attempting to speak. "I used to play in this river with my cousins. In Glasgow."

"Aye. Well, there isn't much playing at the mill, I'm afraid."

"Can I sit up front with you?" he asked, motioning towards the space beside Mr. Chapman.

"Ah, I would love to bring you up front, but as you can see, I'm transporting a very fragile item."

Nicholas leaned forward and spotted a green velvet hat with silver trim. He snorted.

"Snicker all you want, young man. This hat is worth more than anything else in my wagon."

"What's special about it?"

Mr. Chapman glanced over his shoulder at him. "It's not just the hat, it's who the hat is for. An old friend."

Nicholas, not willing to fight a hat for a front seat, sat down on one of the many boxes around him. "What will I be doing there?"

"At the mill? What most boys do. Doffing, I suspect. In time, you'll work one of the looms," he said with a half-laugh.

The River Clyde rushed through bends and over rocks, the vegetation on its banks a bluish-green. Despite the river's constant thrash, it was the mill that captured Nicholas's attention.

New Lanark's Mill stood tall and wide, dwarfing the surrounding structures. The grey bricks of its exterior hummed with industry. It housed hundreds of looms, which pounded a deafening din that filled the structure and spilled out onto the street. Large windows decorated both its eastern and western sides.

When the carriage came to a stop, a phantom buzz at the base of Nicholas's skull replaced the bumpy ride's sensation. He leapt from the carriage onto the street and its familiar stone padding. He winced when he landed, his knees a continual reminder of an accident he wished he could forget.

Nicholas thanked Mr. Chapman before pushing open the heavy front door. It opened to a dusty hallway, the noise of the looms already assaulting his ears. He spied a group of children at the far end of the hall, huddled in a group.

A cracked wooden sign hung to his left.

All Visitors Report to Mr. Camran Munroe

"Hello!" Nicholas shouted. The group of boys didn't hear him over the commotion. Nicholas took a few steps forward and several of them took notice. As he moved closer, they shrank back; one even tripped over the feet of another, stumbling before catching himself. Their faces were grey, no colour at all. The boy closest to him was missing a finger on his right hand. He tucked it into his pocket when he saw Nicholas staring.

"Can you tell me where to find Mr. Munroe?"

One boy stepped forward. Nicks and scrapes covered his scalp, probably from cutting his own mop.

Before the boy could speak, a voice shrieked from behind Nicholas, "Take yer lot and get to the dorm. If ye aren't on my clock, ye should not be on my mind, or in my sight."

The gaggle of children scampered off into another room. Nicholas spun around to come face to face with a man—a very short man. It was rare Nicholas could look an adult in the eye without craning his neck. He wore a little canvas wrap, dulled by time, that, because of his height, touched the floor.

"And you, who are you? Ye don't look like you're with them."

"No, sir, I'm not. I'm Mr. Locherbie's son, Nicholas. He spoke with you about a position."

"A position?" he chuckled. "You don't come to New Lanark Cotton for a position, lad. Ye come here for money. Either because you've worked everywhere else or because it's the first place ye saw. But either way, ye come here for money, not a position. Get that through yer pinhead now and yer life will be a lot less disappointin'."

Nicholas noted that Mr. Munroe's head was the same size as his own.

"You don't talk now? That's good. I have no use for talkers. What I need are doffers." Mr. Munroe grabbed Nicholas's arm and shook it roughly. "This is what I need. Long, thin arms like this one. Come here, I'll show you what you're to do. Don't ask questions 'cause ye shouldn't need to; pay attention 'cause I won't tell ye twice. Take off your shoes."

"My shoes?"

"Aye, take them off. Doffers don't wear shoes."

"Where can I keep them?"

"I don't care."

Nicholas removed his shoes and elected to carry them. The diminutive man led Nicholas into the main area of the mill. The metallic wheels of the looms reflected the morning sun, now high enough to angle a sheet of light through the middle of the building. Women and a few children stood nearby each one; the sunlight split their faces in two halves, one dark, and the other white.

None of the workers acknowledged their presence. Most of them stared straight ahead, expressionless. Their arms worked the controls, consuming raw cotton at a frantic pace. The looms worked with uniform precision, with an exactness and speed no human could match.

Nicholas's mother used to work with cotton from their home. There were similarities, but it was less frantic. He squeezed his fingers against the cuffs of his waistcoat, the last his mother made him.

"This is where you will make your fortune, young man!" Mr. Munroe laughed at a joke only he found funny. "I will pay ye six pence a day and ye will be available for as long as these machines are being run. When the bobbins on each o' the looms are full, they'll stop, ye will hear one of the throstle jobbers whistle. That is yer signal to come and change all the bobbins so we can get back to making money. Until you hear one of my men whistle, you are free to do whatever little boys do, within earshot, of course."

Mr. Munroe smiled. Nicholas didn't know why.

"Come here, stand beside me. I want to show ye something."

Nicholas stepped closer to his new boss and Mr. Munroe put his arm around his shoulders, an awkward position since they were the same height.

"Now, crouch down, get close to the floor."

Nicholas squatted down with the man, putting his leg in some discomfort.

"Now wait for it."

"Wait for wh—"

"Shut yer mouth and wait for it."

Nicholas stayed in this crouched position, a heavy arm on his shoulder, the stink of Mr. Munroe's sweat filling his nostrils, the noise of production surrounding him, his knees aching.

Nicholas had just spent the better part of several months in bed recovering and developed a healthy interest in machines of all kinds. His father brought him small curios from the city to tinker with and encouraged the interest. He'd lose hours staring at them, working out their purpose and how they functioned. That led him here. These devices were the future and Nicholas had a great capacity for understanding how they operated.

Nicholas didn't notice when he slipped into a trance while observing them. The looms and their operators moved in unison, or seemed to, as though all the surrounding motion—mechanical and human—were balancing, aligning in some unseen harmony.

The longer he watched, the more the scene slowed. Movement left trails in his vision. Repeated actions overlapped one another. The sight made it possible for him to count rotations and shifts, and there were thousands of spindles, tens of thousands, spinning in such elegant chaos. He found himself lost like this whenever he focused on some mechanical wonder, the metal revealing secrets to him he could never repeat but which became a certain kind of intuition for understanding its purpose.

It continued to slow almost to a stop.

Captivated, Nicholas almost missed seeing one of the bobbins fall from its place. Not even this moment could strip it from gravity. It struck the shop floor with a crash closer to a pile of bricks than a wooden bauble.

The sound startled Nicholas from his daze.

"There it is!" Mr. Munroe shouted. "Those bobbins. That's what

I need you for. That's what I need your tiny hands for." Mr. Munroe giggled. He reached for Nicholas's arm again and pushed it forward, nodding his head toward the bobbin.

"From time to time, you may see one of the bobbins come loose and fall to the ground. Not only is this money we are no longer making, but it can cause all kinds of nasty problems for the machines. Do retrieve them." He paused. "We cannot stop the looms for every fallen bobbin, so you may have to do this when they are on. Be quick."

"You want me to get it right now?" Nicholas asked.

"Well, if not now, when is a good time for ye, lad? Shall we say in an hour or two?" Mr. Munroe almost looked genuine when he asked.

"I don't know what to do, and it looks like I could get my hand caught."

"Aye, that is a possibility, but this is why you must do so safely. Think of yourself as a specialist, Nickie. Can I call you that?" He didn't wait for Nicholas to respond. "There are many dangers at any job. Your father tells me you were working in a mine before this. Do you think you were any safer there? Worrying about explosives, cave-ins, toxic fumes, any number of buffoons running you down with a cart. Silly business the coal mine is. Only a desperate man would call that a vocation."

Nicholas shot a look at his new boss.

"I'm sure your father has other, nobler reasons. Anyhow, enough chatter, you must get to work. Stay here, play with the other rats, watch for bobbins, get them when they fall. Do not leave the mill until relieved. Do not talk or distract the other workers and, as you pointed out, do be safe."

With those last words of warning, Mr. Munroe sped back from where they entered, his wrap kicking up as it knocked against his ankles.

Nicholas looked back to the loom, its moving parts more

menacing now than they were a moment earlier. There were several children his age stationed throughout the facility. Some even looked as though they were in charge of several. He could see the odd one stepping up to the side of a loom, hands plunging beneath to grab fallen bobbins in one smooth movement. The boy moved as if it were an afterthought. Nicholas couldn't fathom the thought of becoming bored when faced with the chance of losing an arm.

He looked back at the bobbin that taunted him from below and tried to focus on the rhythm of the wheel, the spindles, the gears, the thrashing arms that threatened to catch his hand.

Nicholas braced himself and pulled his arm back, ready to strike.

"Wait. Not now," the woman running the loom said.

With all his focus on the bobbin, Nicholas forgot about the operator. Her drab clothing hung loose around her body.

"Let me slow it down for you. You'll never get it out with me running this thing at full speed. Not even a hummingbird moves that fast." She pulled a few of the levers down, and the wheel of the loom began to slow.

"You still have to be careful, but you should be able to manage it without getting hurt," she said, never removing her gaze from the loom's controls. "It's a shite job you have 'ere. I'd feel sorry for you if you were the only one." She waved a hand in front of her. "As you can see, though, you aren't," she continued. "Munroe could shut the machines down for an hour and have them all swept out, but he doesn't want to stop them, y'see. He loses money when they stop. He loses money when someone gets hurt. He loses money when we slow down. He loses money when our shifts change over. It's a wonder he manages to make any money with all the ways he knows how to lose it."

Nicholas smiled. "My name is Nicholas. What's yours?"

"Meredith. It's a pleasure to meet you, Nicholas. I've an uncle with the same name." She looked at him. "Smart man. Wouldn't catch him dead in a place like this," she smirked. "Give it a try. Go on. That bobbin won't come to you, lad."

Meredith resumed her work, and Nicholas rolled the sleeve of his jacket up to his elbow. He took a deep breath and waited to once again find the rhythm of the loom. He found the perfect moment to plunge his arm in and just as he spotted his opening, he thrust forward and felt his fingers contact the bobbin. Then, the factory went dark. For a moment, he thought the machine had taken him whole, arm and all. He tilted his head back and saw the light pouring in through the windows still.

"What happened?" he yelled.

"Power went out." Meredith pointed at the line shaft. The thick leather belts powering the looms weren't running. "The waterwheel must have stopped. Your lucky day, Nic." Meredith pulled a small package from the pocket on her sleeve and unwrapped it. Two papelates fell out. She motioned to Nicholas.

"Uh, no, thanks," he said.

She smiled, "No, I suppose not."

"So, what do we do now?" he asked.

"You're lookin' at it. And in case you're wondering, no, we won't be paid for this." She struck a match, and the flame lit up her face as she brought it closer to the end of the thin bark that dangled from her lips. The small light swept across her soft features, hidden under the factory grease and grime. A thick puff of smoke obscured her face.

Mr. Munroe stomped throughout the mill, barking orders at people, telling them to check this and fix that.

"Sounds like a big one. They may send us home. Doesn't happen often, but when it does, it's the closest thing to answered prayer, lad." She took a long puff. "It's a shame it happened on yer first day. You won't be learnin' too much, then."

"I'm pretty sure I had it. The bobbin, I mean."

"Thinking you have something and actually having it are two

very different things, child. Especially when it involves tiny fingers."

She tapped the papelate, and a few ashes fell to the wooden floor. She kicked at them with her boot.

Shouting rang from the far end of the building, and they both turned to face it. Nicholas climbed onto a nearby stool for a better view.

"And that's that. Looks like we're free to go, young man. Come back tomorrow and I'll make sure the loom treats you well. Now go. Do whatever it is that boys do."

He did not hesitate.

CHAPTER FIFTEEN

THEY SET sail with a small crew early the next morning. They were not happy when they realised Ned wanted to return to the mainland so soon. They were expecting a long rest through the winter, but were now back on this rickety ship, risking their lives on a hunch. Emma made a handful of the men draw sticks and managed to convince ten of them to abide by the rules.

Ned barely slept and, by the looks of him, neither had James. Ned spotted the old man standing at the bow. His hair was swept back in loose tangles by the rushing wind and he had shed his heavy coat. For a moment, he let the slow bobbing image of the man take on the role of his father and it felt right.

James had shared many things the night before. It made it hard to see him any other way but as a father. None of it had rekindled a memory though. It was information, not yet a life.

Ned joined him and they watched the Shetland Islands pull away.

James broke the silence. "I noticed you no longer limp. A miracle."

"Did I have a limp? That might explain the ache in my legs before a storm."

"Aye, you had one. I never forgave myself for that."

The way his voice cracked when he spoke gave Ned pause enough to let the moment pass.

"It's not easy calling you Ned, son."

He put a hand on James's shoulder. "It'll have to be this way until... I don't know how long it will have to be this way."

They turned as Emma approached them.

"Do I look like a Ned to you?"

"You look like someone who should be cheering up a glum crew." She smirked. "But no, you don't. I quite dislike it, actually. Feels more like a sound than a name. A click of the tongue." She shrugged. "I'm accustomed to it now."

Ned acted offended. "Had I known no one liked the name I would have written to our friends to the south and requested we base our rebellion on someone else. I hear some of them are using Captain Swing. Do you prefer that?"

James chuckled.

"A bit theatrical, but it's exciting to say."

"It's too late now. The authorities already printed up the wanted posters and the name is the only thing they got right."

"No matter. You'd probably make as good a captain as you do a general."

"The very best then."

"Aye, the *very* best. Can I convince you to captain your ship now?" she asked.

"We'll talk more. We have nothing but time now. Tend to your duties," James said.

DESPITE A ROTTEN TEMPERAMENT, the crew docked the ship before the sun rose again. Unfortunately, the time aboard the vessel offered little time for conversation between Ned and his father.

The weather turned poor and the Luddite's skeleton crew meant everyone was on duty to keep them on course.

Finally, they entered the Moray Firth and docked at Inverness, and their route to Edinburgh stretched on. They brought horses, but Whistlejacket was never fond of travelling by sea. It took her a day more to shake off the sea before they could continue south. They stuck to main roads as much as possible. Emma was unworried here. They were three travellers now, not a conspicuous group. She led them to water often, allowing them and their horses to drink and to camp when night came. After several days, they reached the winding River Forth, which they would follow east before reaching the outskirts of the capital.

They were sore and exhausted. Ned worried how James would hold up, but he whistled frequently, which annoyed Emma, but seemed to keep the old man's mood light. Occasionally, a landmark triggered a memory, which he would share with delight. Ned learned more about his supposed mother and family, but with no context of his own, it was all someone else's life, someone else's family. He wanted answers but couldn't formulate the questions.

Ned and Emma spent the evenings with small conversations. James spent his time on his own. He mentioned not wanting to intrude, but Ned suspected that was his way of excusing himself to capture some time with his own thoughts. He often scribbled in a notebook, smoking a pipe. Ned wondered if he would smoke too if he had grown up with his father.

They arrived in the late afternoon and were all eager to find a bed. The air smelled old and wet the closer they came to Edinburgh. The sun burned red hanging against the pink sky, and it bathed their approach to the city in a warmth that none of them felt.

"It's too late to meet the merchant. They'll have gone home long ago. Let's find an inn and we'll start our search in the morning," Ned said.

"I know a place we can stay. An old friend left his home in my care while he's in France," James said.

"You have friends who holiday in France?" Emma asked.

"Not a holiday. He's a government man."

"A government man?" Ned and Emma pulled the reins on their horses. "You want the leader of the Luddites to stay in the home of a man who would hang him?"

James turned his horse back to the pair. "I'm sorry. I didn't consider that."

"It worries me to think about what else you didn't consider," Emma said.

"I assure you it will be safe. No one will know we are there. I'm the only one with access."

Ned looked to Emma for a response. Instead, she asked another question.

"James, what is your occupation?"

"He's a carpenter," Ned said.

"A carpenter? Is that so?"

James nodded.

Emma circled her horse around James, examining him. "For a carpenter, you have remarkably smooth hands."

Ned noticed the muscles in James's jaw clench before he deflated, his head falling down for a moment before he looked them in the eyes again. "I am a sheriff principal."

Emma's hand fell to her sword. "This is a trap, Ned."

"It's not a trap. I am the sheriff principal for Lanarkshire. I am a judge, but I have no intention of reporting you or any of your associates. Please—"

"You told me you were a carpenter. So, you lied to me from the very first moment."

"I'm sorry. When I discovered who you were, I knew if I—"

"We must turn around, Ned. We aren't safe with this man. If he hid this from us, there's no telling what else he may have hidden."

Ned's gaze didn't break from James. He studied him, looking

for the truth in his slumping frame, weathered face. "You must have known this would come out, James. Why bother hiding it from us?"

"You would have killed me the moment I set foot on that beach. Or she would have."

"Aye. Wise choice, because I'm thinking about striking you down right now."

"I know this isn't what you want to hear. I could have continued to lie. Told you anything else, but I didn't. I don't want to lose you again, son. It was a foolish error. No more lies. This is the truth. Now."

Ned leaned forward in his saddle, patted Whistlejacket.

"Ned?" Emma pressed.

A small company of gannets flew overhead, their squawking distracting all three of them.

"I come all this way and I'm still plagued by those damn birds," Ned said.

"Gannets are remarkable birds. They can nest on steep inclines of rock, even with waves crashing around them. Do you know how that's possible?" James asked.

Ned and Emma were silent.

"Their droppings. They can make a nest in the most awkward of places because their droppings fuse to the rock. They build homes for their family and for themselves on a foundation of shit. Nothing is perfect, Ned. This isn't perfect. I'm not perfect and I'm not the man you may have wanted as your father, but I am your father, nonetheless. And if you weren't so busy worrying about being caught, you might have also considered what I'm putting at stake being seen with you. I'm a judge and my son is a wanted criminal. I'm fine with that. Are you?"

Having made his point, James coaxed his horse along the path. Ned and Emma watched him pull away.

"Do you think he prepared that little speech?" she asked.

"He must have."

"I'll admit, it was pretty good," she said.

"Do you trust him?"

"No. Do you?"

"I don't know." Ned reached for Emma's hand and pulled it away from her sword. "I don't think he means us harm, though."

"Yes, sir." Emma said, her formality not going unnoticed.

They caught up with James, who made no sign of satisfaction. They rode their horses through the muddy streets of Edinburgh's Old Town before reaching the Earthen Mound and crossing north into New Town. A second-floor home, it perched above Princes Street, a step up from anywhere Ned had slept before.

James pushed the wooden door open and set about lighting lanterns. White and pink striped the entry. The alternating pattern ran up half of the wall before switching to white marble. Blue veins ran through the great slabs, giving it a smoky texture. Ned placed his fingertips against it to remind himself of how smooth it could be.

"Government work pays well," Emma said.

"You'll find your bedroom upstairs, first door on the left. If you'll excuse me, I have not slept well in many days and my body and mind are quite spent."

"Where is your room?" Emma asked.

"Right across the hall from yours," he paused. "Don't worry, you'll hear me if I try to leave during the night." James left them and walked up the staircase to the rooms above. His heavy steps sent creaks through the floorboards.

Emma walked further in, letting her hand trail behind her along the walls and furniture. The main room held a small table with thick, curved legs. Four chairs surrounded it. The chair backs were a darker wood than the table and each framed a plush, red cushion.

Each piece of furniture was more indulgent than the last. They were tourists here. None of this was a home to him.

Emma pressed a finger onto each polished adornment that

topped each chair like tiny chess pieces. She passed by them with slow steps that made small sounds like a brush against canvas. A slice of moonlight cut across the room, illuminating her silhouette. As she passed through, she created a thousand brilliant moments. Within each, a sliver of her bathed in silver light and she looked as much a part of the room as the dark table and each dark chair.

Ned wondered how she made herself a part of any space. She never wore a dress, but she was royalty, for a moment, and it suited her as all things did.

A large painting hung over the hearth at the far end. A family of four—husband, wife, son, and daughter. She stood in front of the portrait with her head turned up, her right arm bent at the elbow, clutching her left to her side.

The floor creaked as Ned approached.

"A lovely room," he remarked.

"It's a bit shite, if you ask me." She smiled. "I don't want to stay here any longer than we have to. This place makes me uncomfortable." She poked the burned logs in the hearth with her boot. "Feels haunted. Maybe I need some rest."

"Aye, I know I do."

Ned slid his arms around her from behind, resting his chin on her shoulder.

"Tell me we'll never be this, Ned?" she asked, staring up at the portrait.

"We will never be this."

She sighed. "Good."

They slept together that evening and made love like the newly wed in a bed fit for a king and queen. They shook the salt from the sea and the dirt from the road off their naked bodies and when they finished, sweat chilled their skin and kept them huddled together under sheets softer than any they could remember.

CHAPTER SIXTEEN

NICHOLAS SPENT the remaining hours of the afternoon by the river. He stretched his legs out across the wet grass and even though his knees cracked in protest; his muscles relaxed. He dozed off for a spell, the river lulling him to sleep, but a rustle from behind soon stirred him.

"Nicholas! There ye are!" Mr. Chapman had found him. "My, you are a hard one to keep track of. I heard the mill shut down."

"Sorry, Mr. Chapman. I was going to come find you."

"Aye, of course. I spoke with Mr. Munroe. He tells me the mill will be down for at least a few days. I'll take you back to Edinburgh in the morning so you can spend the rest of the week with your family. Tonight, you are my guest. My wife makes an excellent roast stew with only the freshest tatties and carrots and… we have plenty of space. You won't want to leave, I can assure you. Plus, I know my wife would appreciate the company. She's tired of mine," he said with a throaty chuckle.

Despite what seemed to Nicholas as a successful business, the Chapman's lived on the top floor of a modest structure. It lacked many of the intricate flourishes found on buildings in Edinburgh's

New Town and appeared neglected. Ivy covered much of the exterior, and moss and mildew grew in its untended cracks and corners. Despite its state, it was still far nicer than Nicholas's own home.

"It's an old building, Nicholas, but she's stood the test of many seasons. She'll stand for much longer than most of the buildings around here, I reckon," Mr. Chapman piped before entering.

Bright pink thistles perfumed the entryway.

Mrs. Chapman welcomed Nicholas, throwing her arms around him.

"Look at you, wee Locherbie! Well, you aren't wee anymore, are ye?"

"Not anymore," Nicholas replied, embarrassed.

"Come along, now. Dinner's getting cold and a growing boy…" she trailed off as she disappeared into the kitchen.

Nicholas followed and soon found himself ushered to a dining table, staring into a bowl of stew. The warm steam pillowed against his face; the tender orange carrots broke apart against the ridge of his spoon. He took a hearty first mouthful, and the brown broth coated his insides with warmth. The tender meat fell to bits in his mouth along with a chunk of potato.

A good meal always improved his attitude. He sopped the rest of his stew up before letting the spoon fall back into his bowl.

Mrs. Chapman was dressed in plain, clean clothes. Her cheeks were rosy and round, and her hands were thick and rough. She bumped his chair as she cleared the table, moving with the grace of someone who had never set foot in this space before. She hummed a tune while she worked.

"That mill seems to shut down every other week now," Mrs. Chapman said.

"I'm not sure why. Mr. Owen doesn't spare a cent on its maintenance. It must frustrate him to no end to see it all wasted when the river doesn't cooperate."

"Oh, come now, these aren't all coincidences. Everyone knows that awful Mr. Munroe has made more than his share of enemies. Even with all that Robert has done to make the mill safer, it won't ever be enough for some. Ye know that," Mrs. Chapman said as she took a seat at the table again.

"Aye, I suppose yer right, dear," Mr. Chapman glanced towards Nicholas before continuing, "but we need not talk of this now. We have a guest!"

"Aye, how's the stew, lad?" Mrs. Chapman asked.

"It's the best thing I've eaten in years," he said.

Mrs. Chapman smiled.

Mr. Chapman winked at Nicholas. "It wasn't a lie. I'm not sure where she learned how to cook, but it wasn't from her mother."

Mrs. Chapman slapped his arm. Nicholas laughed.

"Well, I don't know about you, young Locherbie, but the trip from Edinburgh always takes the life outta me and we have to do it all again tomorrow. I'm retiring for the evening."

"Goodnight, Mr. Chapman. Thank you for letting me stay the night."

"No worry, lad. It's nice to have another voice around here once in a while. Shockingly, she gets annoyed with mine." Mr. Chapman said, motioning to his wife.

"Aye, shockingly." She smiled and gave her husband a kiss as she passed behind him. "I'll show you where you'll be sleeping, Nicholas. We haven't changed much of Dougie's room yet. It's still very much how he left it. It should suit y'fine."

Mrs. Chapman led him out of the dining room and further down the hallway, past the bathroom and into the second door on the left. There were so many rooms. He wasn't used to the privacy.

"You'll be comfortable here. Some of his clothes should fit you, so I'll lay them out for tomorrow if ye wish to change. I'll leave you to it, though. You know where the loo is. Goodnight, Nicholas." Mrs. Chapman closed the door behind her.

Nicholas stripped down to his undergarments and allowed himself to fall face down onto the cool bed, stuffing his face into the soft pillow for several minutes before turning over onto his back. He stretched out his legs. The relief was immeasurable. He'd met the Chapmans's son once, years ago. He died from sickness of some kind. He tried to remember his face, but failed.

Instead, he thought of his parents, alone at home, his mother no doubt in bed, coughing and sweating from her persistent fever. His father would be sitting by the stove, trying to fit another log inside, shivering even under his heavy clothes.

The dinner and this home made him realise how desperate they were. It did not make him feel good inside. For a moment, he thought he might never want to return at all. That made him feel worse.

The sting of that thought lessened with each breath. His mind drifted away, his stomach full for the first time in months.

CHAPTER SEVENTEEN

THEY WOKE late to the sounds of horses on the street beneath their second-floor bedroom. Ned rolled out from under the sheets to the window and saw the carriage below, the stable hands already bringing the horses out.

"James woke early," Ned said, pulling his dusty shirt over his head.

Emma rustled from her stillness at the sound of his voice.

"Must I join you? Or can I stay here in this wonderful bed?"

"How will you protect me from bed?" he asked, tossing her leather travelling clothes at her.

"Comfortably, I imagine," she said.

"Come on, I want to get this over with."

"Do not worry, my love. I've been awake since James crept from his room. He made tea, then fed the horses. He cannot evade my senses."

Ned chuckled. "You frighten me."

"Good."

The pair dressed and made their way downstairs.

"I didn't expect the two of you for another hour," James called from outside the front door. He raised a grey eyebrow that brushed against his bangs.

"I rarely sleep, James. That's something you can expect."

James ignored the jab. "I thought it might be best to travel through the city with a bit of cover. I arranged for a carriage to pick us up. No sense showing your face in the capital for longer than you have to."

"That is wise," Emma said.

"I'll count that as a minor victory, then. Shall we leave right away?"

"How are you so full of life? You've travelled twice the distance we have," Ned said, climbing into the carriage.

"I don't have as much time left in this world as you lot, Ned. So I take advantage."

Once inside, James rapped his knuckles on the roof and the driver took them along the cobbled streets of New Town.

"Can we talk about what we're doing now?" Ned asked.

"I'll take you to where I found the merchant. He's near Holyrood and we'll be there at a similar time. Someone in the area should know where we can find his shop. Once we find him, it seems to me we leave him alone with Emma. At the very least, I hope she finds me a man of my word."

"It will help, James," she said.

The carriage rolled east down High Street; the musk of manure and livestock near the markets filled the interior. A pig, unimpressed by the passing vehicle, sat motionless in the shade of a rickety stone building, a home to dozens, no doubt. Several women carrying baskets filled with vegetables hollered to passersby, hoping to sell enough to buy their families dinner. A few children, faces fresh with dirt and mischief, threw rocks at the carriage before the driver shooed them away.

"Do you remember the last time you were in the capital, Ned?" James asked.

"It's been years," he responded, his eyes still focused on the activity surrounding them.

"A blessing. There are more than a few things about this city I'd like to forget," Emma said.

"I don't want to stay here any longer than we need to. There are too many ghosts here," Ned said.

They carried on for several more minutes in silence before coming to a stop in front of Holyrood Castle.

James gave instructions to the driver to continue on and circle back in thirty minutes. Ned and Emma stood outside the castle gates, searching the crowds that passed by. Three British soldiers, their red uniforms glowing against the brown stones behind them, caught Ned's attention. He avoided their notice by putting some distance between them and they gave no hint that he had failed.

"We'll find no one in this mess and the longer we're out here, the more worried I am that someone will recognise you," Emma said.

"That shouldn't be a problem. I'm not wearing a single article of women's clothing. They'll never know it's me."

Emma rolled her eyes. "We should have kept the carriage here and left you inside," she said.

"You're right. That's my error." James said.

Emma escorted him to the perimeter of the small square. "Stay here. Don't draw attention to yourself. James and I will find the merchant. Don't leave this spot." She motioned to James to follow her before stopping and turning back to Ned. "Please." She smiled before slipping away.

Ned did not enjoy waiting. If he was going to stand here in the open, why didn't he just stay in bed? Several boys polished shoes nearby. The sharp scent of blacking struck him all at once, forcing him to move a short distance away from his assigned spot. It was this slight shift in position that brought him within spitting distance of warm meat pies. His stomach grumbled. He tried to distract himself with the sound of a bird overhead, a whistle from a man, the laughter from a trio of women. A shop door blew shut, startling him.

"Excuse me?"

A small woman, her back bent, sidled up beside him. She poked his leg with a small stick.

"Yes?" he asked.

She stuck her tongue out between her lips and furrowed her brow. It looked as though she were solving an intractable problem.

"Are you speaking to me, young man?" she asked.

"You spoke to me first."

"Aye."

Ned paused. Not sure how to respond. "Do you want something of me?"

"Aye. Are you looking for the best meat pie ye've ever tasted?"

Ned's shoulders sank. "No."

"Then quit wasting my time!" she cawed, brushing past him.

Behind you.

Ned heard the words as if they'd been spoken inside his own head. He spun around.

Behind him, he saw a round man in fine clothes leaning against the wall of a close hidden in shadow. He stepped towards the stranger and noticed more details as his eyes adjusted. His waistcoat was frayed in several places and mud soiled his pants. A crumpled hat sat atop a sun- and wine-reddened face.

"Excuse me, sir, do you know where I can find a man by the name of Chapman?"

"I do," he said between hiccups.

"Can you tell me where?"

The man lurched forward, stopping himself just before falling, and bent forward as awkward as a marionette in inexperienced hands.

"Mr. Chapman?" Ned asked.

"At your service, lad."

The man's eyes were milky and grey. He stared in Ned's direction, but off to the left. It unnerved him.

"You're blind," Ned said.

"I am. Wasn't always," Mr. Chapman said.

"What happened?"

"Some bloke tackles me in this 'ere alley, touches my forehead," he raised a shaky finger to his forehead and tapped it. "Now I'm blind."

"That sounds..."

"Unbelievable?" he leaned forward like he was going to tell Ned a secret, "That's what my wife said too. And me customers."

"I'm sorry. No matter how it happened."

"Don't have to be. If you're going to cure me, I'll buy you a drink."

Ned looked back to the bustling square, hoping to see Emma. "Cure you?"

"He told me if I gave a man a letter, that the man'd bring someone back to cure me. So here I am. I've been 'ere for weeks. Got here early, but my friends kept me warm." He laughed, pointing to the empty bottles near his feet.

"Who told you to meet me here?"

"He never gave me a name. I didn't get a good look at 'im before he blinded me. You can fix me, though, can't you?"

Ned stepped further into the close, the sounds of the square a dull roar behind him. He pitied the man. His jaw hung open like a hungry dog looking for scraps; his hands waved about, fingers searching for anything to hold on to. Ned offered an arm to support him and at the slightest touch, the merchant collapsed into his chest. He cried and a deep moan filled the alley, loud enough to attract some attention from people close to the entrance.

"Do you know James Locherbie?" Ned asked, trying to avoid answering the fragile man's request. It was pointless though. He continued to wail.

Ned felt for the man, but he needed to know. He shook him at the shoulders. "Listen to me! How did you know who to give the letter to?"

Mr. Chapman stopped crying. He sniffed a few tears away and ran his dirty hand under his nose. "I don't know! He came to me."

"What did he sound like?"

"Older, distinguished even."

"Did either of them say anything else?"

"You're cruel and playing games with me now. You can't help me." He began pulling at his clothes, tearing it further in places. "No, please, you have to. Please, take this... light."

"What light?"

"The light." The merchant raised a fist to his head. "He left it inside," he struck himself, "inside my mind. It burns. Fix me. Please, take it from me." He sucked in air, his breathing shallow and laboured. "Take it!" he screamed at him through bared teeth, saliva dripping down his lip. "Please, take it," he moaned. The skin of his face drew tight as his features pushed to extremes and he began sobbing again. He fell to his knees, grasping at Ned. "Take it, take it, take it, take it," he whispered. "I didn't deserve this. Take it from me."

Ned watched in silence, helpless. "I'm sorry."

Mr. Chapman stood upright again, leaning back against the wall, his face a mess of fluids and loose strands of hair stuck to his cheek, wet with tears and saliva.

Ned stepped back.

"Wait, wait. Don't leave yet. Just touch my head. Touch my head where he did. Here, give me your hand." He extended a filthy palm towards Ned.

Ned looked back at the entrance to the close. Still no Emma, no James. This was their only lead. He couldn't leave this man. He sighed, putting his hand in the merchant's.

"Okay, okay, right here. Put your fingers and your thumb. All five. Like this." Mr. Chapman arranged his fingers into a claw-like shape. "Hold it. Like that."

Ned grasped the man's shoulder with his other hand, steadying both of them. The doctor jumped at his touch. Ned wondered how long he would have to play along to convince him that he could not heal him.

Mr. Chapman's breathing slowed, and a calm washed over Ned. The man puffed his chest and stood taller, like a load lifted from him. Then a light passed over his face, as if a cloud, obscuring the sun, had slid away and let light shine into the alley. Ned looked up. The sun hadn't risen high enough to light this Old Town passage. The creases in the doctor's face were lighter. Ned gasped as the man's eyes transformed from grey to brown, his skin tightened, became supple.

But as the light passed on and over them, so too did a darkness follow. And the darkness did not dissipate as the light did. Ned's world went dark.

CHAPTER EIGHTEEN

Nicholas said his thank-yous and goodbyes to Mrs. Chapman and lay down between the barrels in the back of the wagon to wait for Mr. Chapman to finish breakfast. He heard the distinct smack of a kiss from the couple before Mr. Chapman pulled himself up onto the wagon. It creaked and shook and Nicholas again wondered how it stayed together after so many trips back and forth.

"You back there?" Mr. Chapman shouted over his shoulder.

"I am!"

Mr. Chapman snapped the reins, and the oxen lurched forward, soon leaving New Lanark behind. Nicholas wasn't near as tired as on the way down.

"Mr. Chapman? What is it you do for a living?"

"Hoped you'd ask. I specialise in the very special, lad. Rarities, curios, treasures. I scour the world and sell them at no small cost to those that need or desire them."

"Like pickled cow tongues?"

Mr. Chapman chuckled. "Well, yes, but I sell other things as well."

"Like what?"

"Well, the box back there with you has the mummified head of an Egyptian priest inside."

He turned back to Nicholas, his eyes glinting.

"A what?"

Mr. Chapman laughed again.

"Ye asked, remember? I take orders from wealthy individuals who want to add exotic relics to their collections or from people with a specific trade who cannot find the materials in Scotland to work it."

"Why would someone start a trade they couldn't find the materials for?"

"I'm not sure. But they pay me well to find them, so I don't bother asking."

This was all new to Nicholas, and it didn't sound like a half-bad way to make a living. The Chapmans seemed comfortable, without many worries.

Nicholas eyed the other boxes around him and let his imagination run free with thoughts of what other treasures they held before settling in for the long journey home.

TRAVELLING north was as uneventful as travelling south, and the rest of the trip passed without incident. The carriage rolled into the Grassmarket and Nicholas was as eager to stretch his legs as to get home.

"Nico!" yelled a familiar voice.

Sam sat on a crate only a short distance away, her legs dangling off the side, her heels kicking against the wood in rhythm. She waved to him. She looked older. They hadn't seen each other in months. She visited only once while he recovered from the accident in the mine.

Nicholas jumped from the wagon while it moved. The landing was awkward and painful as his knees reminded him again of his injuries. He waved to Mr. Chapman, who sped along and away.

"Careful there, traveller," she said.

Nicholas squinted his eyes and said, "Are you wearing makeup?"

"Oh, it's so great to see you, Sam. I missed you dreadfully and thought of you often," she said.

"Right, sorry. It is good to see you. I just, I've never seen ye with makeup before. You look so much… like a girl."

"Thanks? That's the nicest thing you've ever said to me, so I'll let it go. I'm working though so I have to go." She pointed at the throng of people in the market.

"You're working in the market?" he asked.

"No, with the gentleman over there. He's buying a few things for a feast at his manor."

Nicholas still didn't know who she was pointing to. "A feast? A manor? Are you married now?"

She punched him in the arm. It hurt. "I just saw you in the wagon and wanted to say hello. It's been so long. I just—Well, I'm just glad I got to see you. Say hello to your family for me, Nico."

"Uh, I will. Sam? Are you—"

Someone whistled from the crowd, and she snapped towards it.

"I have to go! We'll talk again. You need to get home before that storm arrives," Sam said, motioning to grey clouds swelling in the distance. She composed herself before stepping away.

"I like your dress," he said after her.

She turned back and he expected her to lob an insult back. She didn't though. She just smiled and mouthed a thank you, then weaved her way through the market and out of sight.

NICHOLAS WALKED AS FAST as his legs would allow. Thunder punctuated his laboured steps, the air charged and threatening rain with each passing minute.

He passed Sam's home at the fork where a smaller path led towards his own home. A figure stumbled toward him, someone taking an evening stroll to walk off a pint or three.

Leaves fluttered; a chill breeze rolled over Nicholas. He walked the rest of the narrow path towards home. Light flickered from inside. His father was probably putting a tea kettle on.

He pushed open the heavy door. The act felt strange for an instant, as if the night away made him a stranger in this place. He stepped inside, ready to shout for his parents, but instead, his voice cracked.

There, in front of him, his father knelt beside his mother. He held her hand to his head and sobbed. His entire weight lifted with each half-breath. His entirety grew like a shadow to fill the surrounding space before collapsing again. The room glowed orange with candlelight, bathing it in a mood that did not fit the scene.

His mother's body lay still, her eyes closed. Purple veins lay cold and dry under the thin blue-grey skin of her face. Her hair hung weightless off the side of the sofa. Nicholas stared at the space between the ends of her hair and the floor and swallowed hard.

His father wept. He placed her hand on his head and drew it down along his cheek, but it was unnatural.

Nicholas stood in the entryway, paralysed to action.

"Pa..."

The word didn't register with his father.

Everything in the room, the chairs, the tables, the dishes, their bodies, twisted in the flicker of manic shadows. The logs burning in the stove popped and sizzled, air whistling through them to a scream. The very house itself shook with rage.

His father groaned a few unintelligible words that may have just been sounds. Some of them loud, some of them only whispers, all somehow catching in Nicholas's own throat. The sounds were their sounds, or maybe just his own.

Nicholas stepped to his father, stretching out his arm to touch his trembling shoulders. His father recoiled, spinning around to face him, and in one quick motion he wrapped his arm around Nicholas's head, pulling him close.

Pressed against his father's chest, the sour scent of coal burning his lungs again, Nicholas felt something release inside both of them and come loose. Everything at once felt broken; the only remaining woman either of them loved lay still beside them.

CHAPTER NINETEEN

EMMA DARTED through the opening to a tucked away close and her chest tightened. Ned lay against a stone wall, his head hung to the side, his body still.

"Ned! Ned, answer me."

She felt for his breath on the back of her hand while checking him for injuries, but found none, save for a bump on his head where he must have fallen.

James reached them. He froze in place.

"We have to get him back to the wagon."

James stammered, revealing that crisis was not his forte.

"Now, James!"

Her tone set him into motion. He pulled Ned's limp arm over his shoulder, and they brought him to his feet together.

"Can you handle this?"

James nodded. He struggled, but shared the load well enough. They shuffled out of the alley and back into the busy street. Other than a few gawkers, they raised little attention as they passed Ned off as being too eager for drink too early in the day. They laid Ned down on the floor of the carriage and James took a seat.

"Stay here. Don't move."

"Where are you going?"

"I'm going to find who did this."

"How can you—"

"James, look after him. I'll be back soon."

She slammed the door of the carriage and ran to the alley. Crouching, she studied the area. No signs of a struggle. No scuff marks in the dirt between the stones. No scraps of moss torn from the walls. Someone must have snuck up on him. Ned wasn't carrying anything of value. Had his assailant realized this and fled? She spotted a few fresh impressions further into the close where stonework gave way to mud. She followed them to a short set of stairs that led to the backs of homes and forgotten shops. No one made their presence known.

A wren sung from the roof of the building at the far end. It flitted about across several sills.

Emma stared through thick shadows and debris, looking for anything out of place.

"Where are you?" she whispered.

She pulled a dagger from her belt and flipped it over in her hand. Pressing her thumb against a small trigger, the end popped open, the hilt spreading like petals, revealing a small, glass bulb, a swirling amber mist locked inside. She waved it in an arc, watching the bulb's intensity grow as it pointed towards a door on the southern side.

She closed the dagger and replaced it on her belt, drawing a second, less unique one. The door was ajar, a detail she missed on her first pass. She cursed herself before sliding her fingers into the gap and yanking the door open.

She jumped back, stumbling. Light filled the small space, illuminating a figure only a few feet beyond the frame. A man stood, frozen in place, gutted. His organs, exposed to the air, were carved with ghastly precision. The wound, enormous, began at the man's face and went deeper at his gut, before growing shallow at his thighs. It was spherical, as if an animal took one terrifying swipe with a singular giant claw.

The man still stood, somehow. And despite the grisly nature of the crime, his eyes were the most unsettling. Both open, both spared from the gruesome attack. Deep brown pits stared out at her, red with anguish, dried salt gathered at their edges.

CHAPTER TWENTY

NED WOKE to the weakening scent of meat pie, followed by the sound of knocking wood and stone, keeping a steady beat inside his head. Darkness consumed the rest. His skull throbbed.

"Hello?" he spoke into the blankness of his mind.

"Ah, lad. You're okay," James gasped.

Ned didn't need his sight to hear the relief in the man's voice.

"I'm not okay. I can't see! What happened to me? Where's Emma?" his hands fumbled around his surroundings. The carriage jostled him, throwing him off balance.

"Emma is fine, Ned. She's fine," James said. "What do you mean, you can't see?"

Ned felt James's hands on his shoulders, steadying him. He flinched, the sensation unexpected.

"What did he do to me? How is this possible?"

The carriage continued to knock against the stones of High Street as they sped west towards Edinburgh Castle.

"Ned, tell me what happened."

"I don't know. Chapman. He was blind, a madman. He told me to touch his head and I… I went blind."

"Fascinating."

"Fascinating? That's your response?"

"I'm sorry, Ned. That's not what I meant."

"He didn't know what happened, either. He didn't know…"

"Didn't know what?"

"Where's Emma?"

"She stayed behind to pursue whoever did this to you. We found you lying in the close. No one else around. I understand you're scared, but please, you must tell me everything that happened if we're going to figure this out."

"He was a lunatic, James. What happened to me?"

"I'm sorry, lad. I am. This does not sound like the man I met."

Ned pulled himself up onto the seat beside James. He tried to calm himself with deep breaths, but his chest tightened, his entire body trembled, his breathing remained shallow. Emma could have coaxed him out of this state.

The carriage came to a stop in front of their lodging. James exited and helped Ned to the street. They walked arm-in-arm with slow, measured steps. Once inside, the pair made their way upstairs and James helped Ned into bed.

"Don't leave me alone."

"I wouldn't think of it."

Ned's hand swung through the air as he searched for James.

"I'm right here. I'm right here."

Ned propped himself up against the headboard and closed his eyes. James sat beside him. The ticking of a clock downstairs counted the moments that passed.

"Eht tseb dial semehcs fo ecim dna nem..."

"What?"

"It was a game we used to play."

"A game?"

"Aye. We would say things backwards and let the other try to say it forward."

"You're playing a game?"

"I thought it might distract you."

"Distract me? I can't ignore complete darkness, James. I can't see! Forget your games. You aren't even my father. You're a liar and I'm a fool."

"Ned..."

"I don't know what's happening to me, but I know you are not an honest man."

For a long while, they remained quiet. Ned felt the empty air weighing on them both.

"I am sorry. I am your father, but I fear I am quite out of practice." James rose to leave. He took slow steps away from him, followed by the squeak of door hinges as it opened.

"The best laid schemes of mice and men. Robbie Burns."

"Ned, I—"

Floorboards creaked from downstairs, followed by the sound of rushing feet.

"Ned!" Emma called.

"I'm here," he replied.

Emma dashed through the door, pushing James aside.

"I'll let you watch over him," James said.

"You'll not let me do anything, James. I told you to wait. I'll speak with you later," Emma said.

He left the room without a word.

She ran a hand across his cheek, stroked his brow with her thumb.

"What's wrong with you?" she asked.

"I met the merchant. He was blind. Now… now I am."

She cursed. "How is that possible?"

"I have no idea what's happening to me."

"Why did I leave you? So stupid. I thought you'd be safe in the open." She pulled his head towards her, cradled him against her chest.

"Did you find him? Mr. Chapman?" he asked.

"I believe so. Dead."

"Dead? What happened to him?"

"I don't know. I don't want to know."

"Emma, he knew nothing. He was wild, unhinged. Someone hurt him, put something inside him," Ned paused, "Is the door closed?"

"Aye."

"He'd never heard the name James Locherbie."

"We're going to keep this between us until we learn more. I will not leave you alone with him again."

Emma lay beside him, and he fell into her lap.

"Emma..."

"Yes?"

"I'm scared. Everything is black. I can hear things."

"What things?"

"Just, more. I hear more."

Sleep crept up on him with a soft touch; his waking world now looked no different from his resting one.

CHAPTER TWENTY-ONE

NICHOLAS WASN'T sure when or how he fell asleep the night before. He peeled the stiff bed sheet off and sat up, pausing before setting his still-stockinged feet onto the floor.

He hoped with everything in him he would leave the bedroom, only to find his mother and father speaking in hushed tones to one another over a cup of tea. The way they used to. Before last night. Before her sickness. Before the coal mine. Before his sister.

For a split second, his mind played a cruel trick as a woman's voice drifted in from the main room. It didn't last though. The voice was ancient and slow. It was Agata, which meant only one thing.

Nicholas stood at the entry to the main room and spied on the conversation.

"Did ye clean her?" she asked.

His father nodded, staring at the wooden floor, his gaze burrowing into the grain of the wood, the space between the grain of the wood, like he wanted to hide himself there, away from all of this. He swayed, only noticeable because he sat in front of the window, his back to the light. His outline rocked in a steady rhythm.

"I know you wanted to keep her here in your home, but you understand why we moved her?"

Agata's tone was firm, like his mother's, when she explained the way things are, not how Nicholas wished them to be. She was the eldest woman in the hamlet and these responsibilities fell to her. Always the first to arrive when anyone passed, the older children used to scare the younger ones with tales of Agata waiting outside their doors.

"Both you and Nicholas have lost much already; there's no need to delay the burial."

His father didn't respond.

Agata placed her hand on top of his father's head, and he fell forward. A spasm of sound burst from his throat before he choked it back. Agata pulled him in, resting his enormous frame against her.

Nicholas couldn't watch his father break again. He retreated to his bedroom, slipped on his shoes, and left through the window. He rolled over the frame as he did, snagged his coat on an errant nail, a small tear. The sun burned his eyes.

His neighbours rushed about, making preparations for a burial, news of the death having reached them. Several men carried a cooling board into a small structure the hamlet used for viewings. His mother's body lay on top of it. There were too many men around the board. Their limbs blocked his view but framed her dress. It was blue. There were white flowers on it. The same flowers he used to trace with his finger while curled up on the pew beside her when she used to talk to God.

He circled around the commotion to the back of the bothy, where shrubs and branches would hide him. This is where he and Sam witnessed all rituals, through a small crack in the wood, death framed by knotholes and splinters.

The men laid his mother on a table in the centre of the room to prepare her for viewing. Agata entered the structure moments later carrying a wooden bowl and approached his mother's body. The men moved back to the perimeter of the room.

Agata drew a candle from the bowl, struck a match, and lit it. She let the flame flicker for several seconds before extending her arm and proceeding to wave the candle over the body, from head to toe, three times. She blew the candle out and placed it on the table.

Raising the bowl again, she ran her fingers through the salt inside. She lifted a small amount of it and let it slide back into the bowl before placing it onto his mother's chest.

The last time he was here, Sam remarked how much easier it was to balance a bowl on a body that isn't breathing. The thought offended him now.

Agata turned to one man and nodded. Two of them grabbed a length of rope and tied it across his mother's shoulders and legs, binding her body to the board.

One man whispered to Agata and pointed towards his mother, and she pursed her lips in response.

Agata approached his mother again and rolled up her sleeves. It wasn't until then that Nicholas noticed his mother's arms. They bent at disgusting, impossible angles, curled like a dead spider.

Agata gripped one of them and with a single jerk, snapped it at the elbow, snapped it again at the wrist. She lay the arm down across his mother's stomach, now malleable and soft, submissive.

Then another crack, then another crack, then finally a snap, the second arm more stubborn. Once the elbow broke, the wrist offered little resistance. Agata posed his mother like a doll, as if she were only sleeping. This side of her face was smooth, younger than any day before.

The sounds of his mother's arms breaking echoed through him. There was a sharpness to it, followed by a sickening crunch as the bone came loose under the skin. He heard it again, clear as if they were breaking for the first time.

Snap. Snap. Snap.

Nicholas vomited in the surrounding bushes.

Agata and the men left the bothy. Nicholas recovered and snuck around to the front and slid inside without notice. He stared at his mother, now with nothing between them. The stillness of death unnerved him. Making a body that once lived and moved become fixed was somehow more static than if she had never moved at all. The elimination of movement made her seem so much more still than the world around her.

His feet dragged across the dusty wood as he approached her. He leaned over her, brushed his fingers along her stiff arm. Her skin was pale blue, like bruised fruit. He touched her dress, the stiff fabric brushed against his fingers. He found it difficult to look at her face. She did not look like herself, more a stranger who reminds you of someone you know.

Why did he come here? Why did he taint his lasting image of her?

Dust drifted from the roof of the bothy and settled on her. The earth wanted her.

He hated everything at that moment. He hated his life, and he hated that he no longer had a mother. He hated his father for sending him so far to work. He hated Agata for breaking his mother's arms. He hated the ropes across her chest, and he hated the dust for trying to claim her.

And in this flash of emotion, something passed from him and into his mother.

Fix her.

Her chest rose.

He stumbled back, only realising now how tight his grip was on her arm. Everything went quiet around him, and he swallowed hard.

The dust continued to drift from above; the light continued to fall across her body. The wind, blowing through cracks in wood and stone, continued to blow. She didn't move again.

Maybe she never moved at all.

Nicholas stared at his mother, unblinking. Part of him wanted to go back to his bed and lie down. Part of him wanted to touch his mother again.

He did neither of these. Instead, he surprised his own impulses and left.

The world appeared dull. From the outside, his home looked no different from the rest. Any or all of them could hide the horror of another dead mother, another dead wife.

A gannet flapped its wings above him. It was gliding through the air, putting forth little effort. Nicholas imagined himself up there, flying above everyone and everything, making this hamlet so much smaller.

He turned his back on his home and understood what his father had been staring at earlier. It wasn't a space he wanted to hide in. It was the spot he spent his last moment with his wife. These were last moments being conjured, lived again, extending her life, as Nicholas now did against a green and brown backdrop. He thought about her dress, and it was so. He thought about her hair and her skin and her laugh and her heart, and it was so. The illusion was so fragile he dared not move for fear it might break. His mother sat before him, Nicholas at once in front of her and at once curled up beside her. His tiny finger traced the edges of white flowers, and they were suddenly the saddest thing he'd ever seen. But he didn't cry.

It wasn't like this when his sister died. He cried then. This was different. It left him hollowed and scraped out. The woman who brought him into this world was no longer part of it.

And this still hurt less than the realisation that his mother died while he was away. While he slept in a stranger's home, filling his belly with their food, his mother lay in sweaty, stained sheets on a mattress so thin the hard wood of the frame beneath pressed against her. She was covered with sores, leaking and drying to the coarse sheets, peeling open with fresh hurt every time she rolled over to relieve the pain. That was her every day in the last weeks.

And he remembered the moment before he fell asleep at the Chapman's when he thought about not going home.

Deep inside his tiny chest, which heaved at these thoughts, a tiny black seed of guilt formed in the space left open by his mother: she never knew where her only son was as she slipped from this world.

That thought propelled him away. He didn't want to be anywhere near this. He ran on aching legs all the way to Edinburgh.

CHAPTER TWENTY-TWO

SUNLIGHT PASSED THROUGH THE WINDOW, warming Ned's skin. Even without his sight, he knew it was morning.

"Emma?"

"I'm here," she said, as if she had waited all night for him to speak.

Ned ran his hand under the sheets, searching for her. He brushed her bare leg with his thumb and forefinger and pinched it.

"James thinks we should leave the city, get back to the island," she paused for a moment, finding his hand with hers, "But if you're not ready, I'll tell him so."

"How the hell am I going to get from here to the island?"

"I'll help you."

Ned took a deep breath.

"I suppose there's no difference between being useless in bed here or useless in bed there. How will they react when they discover their general is blind?"

"You don't go on raids, so your role doesn't have to change a lot. I'll be your eyes until you regain yours."

"And if I don't?"

"You will," she responded, her tone firm.

"Emma, you don't—"

"Then I will carve out that liar's eyes!" she growled, her composure crumbling.

They said no more after that. Both were on edge.

With Emma's help, Ned dressed and made his way downstairs. Once outside, Ned heard James's footfalls as he approached.

"This will work," Ned said to the open air.

"What will work?" James asked, stepping out of the carriage to greet them.

"The cane."

"What cane?" Emma asked.

"This one, the one you handed..." Ned trailed off. He squeezed his fingers together in a loose fist. "I could have—"

"... swore I gave you a cane?" James asked.

Ned's shoulders fell. "Aye."

"Stranger yet is the fact that I was about to give you one."

Ned felt the polished wood placed in his palm. He ran his fingertips along its length. There were shallow grooves along its body, and an ornament on the head of the cane.

"What is it?" Ned asked.

"The ornament? A flower or a plant. Holly, I believe. I found it inside." James stepped back from the pair, and the carriage door squeaked open. "I took the liberty of leashing our horses to the back of the carriage. I can pay for the driver to take us where we need to go. It will be slower, but I think best considering your condition."

"Thank you, James. Emma, can you—"

"Don't worry, Ned. I gave Whistlejacket a carrot. She'll be fine."

Ned squeezed her arm.

"Shall we leave then?"

The ride was again uneventful, or so it seemed to a newly blind man. Wheels struck stone before giving way to mud and dirt. Smells changed too. Heather, the chirping of chiffchaff, the calls of early snow buntings, the heavy musk of animal waste all drifted through these parts. Emma's knives rang off one another as the carriage bounced along. James cleared his throat an annoying number of times. Some details were pleasant, others irksome.

It wasn't until the path turned into a forest that he experienced his favourite sensations. The air was still, and with it, the surrounding sounds slowed and froze. A willow warbler sang a song that he heard with such precise isolation Ned could have led them all straight to it. A knothole wheezed like an old man when wind rushed through it. The bubbling and splash of a nearby stream tickled his ears as the water rolled over small, smooth stones.

And yet, even with all the noise, he still heard the nervous stamps of hooves somewhere beyond. A horse shuffled under the weight of its rider and let out a small snort, agitating several other horses. The bits of metal on the saddle riggings clinked from their origin to the carriage.

"There are men on horses nearby," Ned said.

"How do you know that?" Emma asked.

"I can hear them. I can hear everything. They're not moving."

"Travellers like us, I'm sure," James offered.

"They have weapons. I can hear their leather gloves squeaking against their hilts."

"You can hear their gloves on their hilts?" Emma asked, her doubt palpable.

"It's beautiful," Ned said. In the blackness of his mind, white lines formed around him. They appeared random at first, reaching out from where he stood and stretching out at awkward angles. The lines were fuzzy and shifted when he tried to focus on them. They connected and intersected, weaving intricate designs he couldn't understand. It wasn't until he made out James's silhouette that he realised he was seeing the world around him, or a version of it. There was no colour, and the beams pulsed, like they were breathing or beating, making it difficult to discern one object from another. He looked to his right and made out Emma's form looking in his direction.

"Ned?" she asked.

The shapes in his mind moved at random intervals. James and Emma were sitting in the carriage with him at one moment, the next they would be ahead of him, further down the road. They were outside of their transport and yet, still sitting. Then their forms would snap back to their original, actual positions. Ned also moved, suddenly ahead of the group, floating above the path, until the rest caught up with him and continued.

"I don't know what I'm seeing," he said.

No time to figure it out either. The next few moments were filled with the chaos of light overlapping and rolling inside his head. He made out several shapes as men on horses. They charged hard towards them and sped up at unbelievable speeds before slowing down again into a near standstill in mid-gallop, floating above the ground just beyond Ned's reach.

One man near the back of the pack drew his sword.

"They're attacking!" Ned shouted, making himself low inside the carriage.

"Who?" Emma asked, kneeling beside him, her hand on his shoulder. "Ned?"

Her voice entered his mind like a muted explosion. The word rippled through the flurry of light lines in front of him, distorting the image further.

Ned took a few quick breaths. The image reassembled again, and the riders retreated now, or rather, they moved backwards, their horses galloping in an impossible manner. The man who drew his sword sheathed it and in one instant, the entire pack withdrew from his sight into the distance. Their forms merged with the faintest light at the edge of all he could see.

The carriage continued to roll through the woodland and the stillness of the surrounding forest returned.

"Ned? What's wrong?" It was Emma's voice.

"I'm not sure," he answered, feeling his way back to his seat. "I saw things. Light. Shapes. You and James, men on horseback attacking us."

James knocked on the roof. "Is anyone on the path ahead of us?" he asked the driver.

A brief pause, then an answer, "No. Emptier than a kirk on Friday, it is."

"Something strange happened to them, to us. We moved forward and backward, occupying many places at once. One moment I was in the carriage, the next I was further down the path. The men were upon us, swords drawn, and then they vanished, pulled back down the road."

A heavy silence entered.

"I can hear you looking at one another," Ned said.

"Ned, neither of us would say you didn't see what you claim, but it is strange," Emma said.

"I know."

"Could it be old memories playing out in your head or a vivid daydream?" James asked.

"No, I wish you were right, James, but you aren't." He paused; the carriage slowed. "Our driver knows it now, too."

The driver bellowed back, "Mr. Locherbie, sir? There's a group of men on horseback approaching. Should we continue or wait and let them pass?"

Emma leaned out of the window. "Eight of them. Dressed in black."

"Merchants," James said.

"All armed."

"Merchants with security?"

"They're not merchants. They're bounty hunters," Ned said. "You're looking at one another again."

"Since you seem to know more than we do, what do we do?" Emma asked.

"We wait. We wait until the one at the back of the pack draws his sword."

"Then we fight," Emma said, gripping the knives at her belt.

"No. Then we know I've not gone mad as well as blind."

CHAPTER TWENTY-THREE

Nicholas hobbled into Edinburgh's Grassmarket, the sound of snapping bone haunting his steps. Not even the bustle of the market could drown it out. He wandered the market, weaving between the cattle and goods.

"Five pence! Those won't last the trip home! You're gonna have to do better," a large man wearing bright-coloured clothes shouted nearby. His voice was smooth, like cream, and his accent exotic. Nicholas stumbled away, trying not to disturb anyone. He collided with a gallows. Nicholas looked up, but saw no one attached to it. Aside from being the liveliest market in Edinburgh, it also doubled as a prime location to hang criminals, though Nicholas couldn't remember the last time that happened. His mother never wanted him to witness a hanging. Sam, on the other hand, snuck away and always returned with horrifying details. It often gave him nightmares.

"This is as fresh as you're gonna get unless ye fish them from the Fyfe yerself. Best fish in all Edinburgh, it is."

"I will trust you at your word, friend. But if they are not, I will be back, you can be sure."

"Well, then I hope I dunnae see ye again. Until you're hungry, of course," the fisherman chuckled.

The exchange shook Nicholas from his thoughts, and he left the pair to their business. He pulled himself up onto a ledge to observe the chaos, the teeming thrash of commerce. He felt invisible here, and he liked that.

Nicholas then spied a curious individual. Sitting on horseback on the eastern edge of the market, a man in black, his face covered. From the fine hairs of its hooves to its mane, his horse shone a brilliant white, popping against the pale browns and dark greens behind it.

The rider's long, black duster hung over the sides and back of his steed. Steel buckles adorned the coat, some tying off pockets, while others seemed less like utility and more like decoration. His face hid behind a high collar that rose a few inches above his ears, the rest was obscured by a three-peaked hat—also black.

Even from this distance, Nicholas felt the rider's eyes on him. He looked left to right, wondering if the man was looking at something beside him. No, he was looking at Nicholas. The man nudged his horse and trotted to his right, heading up the hill towards West Bow. He glanced back before moving from sight as the street curved upward and away.

Follow him.

The words hurt. Was something burning? He thought of the time he watched his uncle brand his cattle. The smell of searing flesh returned to him, but briefly. Nicholas couldn't protest. He didn't want to. The rider had intrigued him. Distracted him. He descended back into the market's madness, quickening his pace as best he could. Breaking through the crowd at the end of the square, he rested his aching legs before limping off in the rider's direction.

The West Bow was home to several shops more amiable to

colour, their storefronts often using purples, reds, and bright blues. None of which seemed commonplace anywhere else in the city. He hadn't noticed this before, but it'd been a while since he'd been here.

Nicholas lumbered past the shops, heading to High Street, the road connecting Edinburgh Castle up the hill, to Holyrood Castle at the bottom. It was a busy intersection, being the primary artery connecting the two ends of Old Town. Upon reaching the top of West Bow, he panned the crowd.

A fog rolled in, making it difficult to distinguish people from one another. There were also several men on horses on High Street, adding to the challenge. Dodging the congestion, Nicholas spotted the rear half of a white horse heading into a tight close.

He crossed the street and peered into the cramped space—Lady Stairs Close. How did a horse squeeze through here? Nicholas had been in Makar's Court before, where this close led. Many of the poorer families, larger than Nicholas's, lived in the cramped spaces here, filling single rooms with eight, ten, sometimes twelve people.

Surrounding Makar's Court were small tenements stacked on top of one another. An unseen host likely watched through windows, witnesses to an unlikely meeting.

The fog eased into the space and grew thickest around the horse. It snorted, a puff of warm air escaping its nostrils added itself to the fog.

Nicholas stepped forward; the rider did not retreat. They were in the centre of the court now. The horse, glowing against the dull air around them, held Nicholas's attention above all else. He stretched out his arm, showing his open palm before turning it over and reaching toward the animal.

Nicholas brought his hand around to the side of the horse's head and let it rest there. A long, white mane fell down the length of its neck, chunks of it clinging to a loose braid that needed some attention. He ran his fingers through the fine hair on the animal's head.

"You are not as I thought you would be," the rider spoke, his voice closer to a ghastly whisper.

"Do I know you?" Nicholas asked, staring at the man, his face still unknowable.

"No, but you will."

"Who are you?" As the words left his mouth, he felt a warmth on his upper lip. His nose was bleeding. Then a great pressure squeezed his temples, bringing him to his knees. His head filled with pain, as if he never knew a moment without it.

Nicholas spat a few inaudible words into the fog as he fell forward.

CHAPTER TWENTY-FOUR

THE SOUND of horses and men barking orders at one another overwhelmed the carriage.

"Tell me what the man at the back is doing?" Ned asked.

"Nothing, he's watching the others," James said.

"No, wait, he drew his sword," Emma said. "Like you said he would. He's pointing it at the driver now. What does this mean? How did you know this would happen?"

"I'm not sure what any of this means, but that's as much as I saw. What comes next? I don't know. What are they doing now?"

"They're forming a half-circle to the left of the carriage," Emma said. She pushed Ned closer to the floor of the carriage. "Keep your head down."

"I've never known bounty hunters to form hunting parties," James said.

"Me either. The reward split can't be favourable. They're all wearing uniforms. All black gear, masks, black riding capes with red lining. Longswords at their hips, crossbows on their backs. These are no ordinary bounty hunters."

"Who are you?" Emma shouted.

"We're here to take General Ned Ludd into custody. Hand him over and the rest of you may leave."

Emma swore. "They're holding your wanted poster."

"You didn't answer our question. Who are you?" Emma repeated.

The man spoke again, but did not answer. "Sarah?"

Emma crumpled, her body launched against the wall of the carriage, forcing the door open. She tumbled out into the grass below.

Ned's world lit up again. The light lines returned, painting his surroundings, giving him sight. Emma already righted herself.

"What happened?" Ned asked.

"One of them shot me. I've never seen someone loose a bolt that fast."

"Are you okay?"

"I'm fine. It didn't go deep, my armour kept it out. If she wanted to kill me, she could have."

The scene replayed for Ned. Emma flew back into the carriage, the woman on the horse, Sarah, drew the crossbow from her back with one arm, the other pulled a bolt from a pouch that hung off the side of her horse's neck and loosed it, sending Emma to her current position. It played out in an instant, filling in the gaps he'd missed.

Watching Emma fall again, even if only he could see it, was two times too many. She was out of danger now, hiding behind one of the carriage's wheels.

Heightened sounds made it difficult for Ned to filter out the useless ones. Even his own breathing was hard to distinguish from those around him. He moved towards the open door.

"Stay down," James said, putting a hand on Ned's shoulder, a surprising amount of strength behind his grip. Ned didn't fight it.

Emma wrapped her fingers around the shaft of the bolt in her shoulder and yanked it out, throwing it into the dirt with a curse.

Ned could see everything now. He could see the carriage

interior, but also through it, to Emma and the riders. The beams of light that made up his world shimmered and reacted to sound, their edges pulsating with every yelled word and each shift in weight.

Emma leaned against the wheel and drew two of the small daggers from her belt. Each long, thin, like fingers. The grips were unlike any other—metal rings designed to control the amount of spin when thrown.

"Emma, wait!"

"No more waiting. If they want to leave with you, then they'll have to kill us all. They're going to anyway, Ned. Keep your head down. They will not like this."

She took a quick breath and let her right arm loose around the back of the carriage, releasing both knives as she did.

Thin strips of metal flashed through the air, slicing through a yellow pole of light breaking through the forest's ceiling. The woman reacted as fast as before, raising her weapon. The first knife, having not completed its arc, glanced off it and fell into the foliage beyond. The second knife did not. Having manoeuvred her crossbow upward, the second knife sliced into her stomach, lodging itself deep inside. She buckled over on her horse.

The rest of the men pulled their bows from their back and began to fire bolts at the carriage, trying to hit Emma before she could let loose any more knives. It was relentless. Ned saw the bolts firing, thudding into the side of their transport, whistling through the windows.

They struck the driver several times, his limp body fell from the seat to the path almost going unnoticed in the carnage.

It was only a matter of time before the riders came around the far side to strike down Emma. She wouldn't be able to fight them all.

"I'm coming out!" Ned shouted.

"Ned!" Emma yelled.

"Emma, I don't doubt your skill, but there are still seven of them. We have few options."

"If I can untie one of our horses, we can make a break back to the city. We can lose them there."

"Three of us aren't going to fit on a horse, Emma."

"He's on his own," she said, motioning to James.

"No, I'll go with them. You and James take our horses and follow from a distance. We'll be easy to track. I'll make sure of that."

"Ned, you can't even see. You can't defend yourself."

"I can't explain it to you, Emma, but I do see. It's different, but I do see."

"Now." The man on horseback ran out of patience.

"If you're leaving, Ned, you better go," James said.

"Yes, Ned, listen to your father. So concerned about your well-being that he's willing to hand you over to bounty hunters to save his pitiful life. However it ends, Ned, don't forget this. He didn't protest once."

"That was not my inten—"

Ned rapped his cane against the door before pushing it into the earth below. "I'm coming out!"

Emma touched his arm. She whispered, "You're a fool, Ned, but I will save you. No matter how difficult you make it."

"I know," he said with a hesitant smirk, and handed her the cane.

Ned walked out to the horsemen with his arms raised.

"Search him."

One of the men approached and checked his belt for a sword, but found nothing. He rifled through his pockets, empty.

"May I ask where you got that poster? I seem to be missing mine," Ned asked.

"Shut your mouth. You'll ride with me."

Ned clicked his tongue, and the sound stretched out from him, painting his surroundings in light. He smiled up at the man and took his outstretched hand.

"You, stay behind. Make sure no one follows you."

With Ned on the back of a horse, the hunters, save two, one having bled out in her saddle and the other itching for revenge, left Emma and James behind.

CHAPTER TWENTY-FIVE

EMMA EYED the bounty hunter left to ensure she didn't follow. He cleaned the dirt from under his fingernails with a knife. "So, what are we doing here, exactly?"

"To be honest, I was hoping you'd turn around and walk in that direction, save me the trouble of guttin' you and yer grandfather, 'ere," he said, pointing back to Edinburgh with the tip of his dagger.

"You're bounty hunters?"

"Well, aren't you an observant cow."

"Then I assume you're the most expendable, is all."

"What are you on about?"

"Well, they left you behind. You must be the least useful."

"They left me behind because they trust me to tie up loose ends, woman."

"Right, of course." Emma approached the rider and pet his horse. "I'm a naturally untrusting person. If they left me behind, I'd think they were going to cut me out of the reward."

The rider looked back down the path where his partners had gone and that's all the window Emma needed. In one fluid motion, she slipped past the horse's head, braced a foot on one of its stirrups, and heaved herself up where she wrapped her arms around the man's neck and pulled him down. They landed in the dirt, he under her. The knock loosened her grip, and he scrambled to his feet, pulling a second dagger from his belt.

He spit. "I was gonna let you go. We're well past that now."

Emma leapt to her feet but drew no weapon to defend herself. She showed her hands. "I wanted to play down here, is all. It's no fun with you way up on that horse."

He lunged toward her, swinging an arm. She stepped aside, the dagger missing. He tried again. She slipped past him, kicking the back of his knee as she did. He sank, but regained his footing.

"We can do this all day, but I'd rather not. I propose a game."

"What kind of game?"

"We throw punches until one of us drops. The winner gets to leave in whatever direction they choose."

The bounty hunter glanced at James. "Is she mad?"

"Aye, I believe she is," James agreed, stepping well out of the range of the pair.

"No dodging, no running, no tricks?"

"Wouldn't dream of it," Emma said.

The man sheathed his daggers and rolled up his sleeves. "My arms are wider than your body. You'll feel every inch, I reckon."

"I don't doubt it. So, do we have a deal?"

"Aye, we have a deal. I'll even let you punch first, since I'm such a gentleman."

Emma curtseyed, then squared her body towards him. "Your wife is a lucky woman."

"Aye, she never complains," he said.

"And why would she? I'm sure you'd beat her within an inch of her life."

"She's earned a smack or two over the years."

The pair circled one another. Emma relaxed her stance and

took slow, sure steps towards him until she was an arm's length away.

He sneered, towering over her. She stared up at him, her eyes narrow, breathing steady and quiet.

She rammed her palm straight up into his jaw. He hadn't been expecting something so fast, straight from below. His teeth crunched, and he staggered back. He spit, blood spattered the grass.

"Ach, I bit my damn tongue!" He spit again. He growled and shook off the pain. "Not bad, but it's my turn. You won't get another one."

"Show me then."

"You won't get a chance to," he grumbled.

"Go on. Hit me like I'm your wife, coward."

He pulled his arm back, and Emma planted her feet as his fist came down on her face. It smacked with a dull spank. Emma's head whipped to the side, absorbing the hit as best she could, but it still dropped her to the ground. She got her arms underneath her, saving her head from meeting the dirt.

She scrunched her face, everything still there, nothing broken, just bleeding. Groaning, she lifted herself to her feet.

"You're a witch. That should have knocked you clean out."

Emma pushed her hair behind her ear, revealing an already bruising eye and cheek. Blood poured from her lips.

"Not a witch. Just a survivor, you bloody madge," she said.

He grunted back.

"I've survived men far worse than you. The type of man so depraved in his tastes and efficient in his indulgence of them, he had to dream up new ways to torture me. And when he wasn't forcing me to take part in his twisted appetites, he would loan me to his friends to rape. At least they lacked his imagination."

She reached into a pouch hanging off her belt and produced a small metallic rod wrapped in leather strips.

"So, you're just the shit on the heel of real nightmares."

The man straightened himself, breathing harder now. "We'll see how you handle another round."

"Then I'll take my time getting there," she said. "One of his friends almost killed me. So he taught me how to defend myself. Not because I was precious to him, but to protect his investment. If I was to be bruised and beaten, it would come from his hand and no other. I learned how to kill a man with my hands. I learned how to kill a man with a blade. I learned how to kill a man," she slid a finger up the inside of her thigh, "in other ways."

She paused again and reached into a second pouch for a curved blade covered in similar leather strips.

"I said no tricks!"

"So stop me."

He wobbled as he tried to step towards her, sweat dripping into his eyes.

She brought the blade together with the handle and with a quick twist, it clicked as it locked into place. She peeled the leather strips away and wrapped them around her wrist.

"What's happen—"

"And with all that training, do you think I could stop him from finding me in my bed, touching what wasn't his to touch? At least before the training I could hide in the luxury of my weakness, but he took that from me, too. He found my only haven and took it away. It was all another sick game to him. He wanted me to know that no matter what I did, it would never stop. But it did."

The man gurgled something back through a clenched jaw, thick saliva forming at the corners of his mouth.

"I didn't quite hear that. Are you having trouble moving? That would be the poison."

Emma bent down and lifted from the dirt a thin razor connected to a small mouthpiece she had held between her teeth. She raised it up between two fingers so he could see it.

"I may not be the only woman you've ever hit, but I'll be the last."

Emma pushed him back with little force, his legs buckled beneath him. He fell with an awkward crunch, and she leaped on top of him, pinning his arms above his head.

"I'm sorry, lad. You drove me to it," she whispered into his ear.

Then, gripping the knife, she slashed down onto his wrists. The first cut produced a glut of blood. She continued to strike the same spot, pushing the knife through muscle and tendon before chipping into the bone. She screamed into his face, louder with each swing, until both hands were severed from his wrists.

His eyes went red, the blood vessels bursting, screams choking in his throat. Blood pooled around his head as he bled out from the stumps. The entire time, he was unable to move, helpless, gasping for air as his body shut down.

She rolled off him, coughing and sputtering, her lungs near bursting in her chest. She rose to her knees and pointed at James, who stood stunned at the edge of the path.

"Get our horses."

James stumbled towards the animals, but couldn't take his eyes off the man, struggling to breathe as he took the reins in hand. "Why don't you kill him? Put him out of his misery."

"It'll be over soon," she said.

Emma moved their packs from the carriage to the horses. "Let their horses go," she said.

James slapped the rear of the rider's horse to shoo him away.

Emma pulled the female rider off to do the same with her horse. She hit the ground and her mask slid off, revealing her face.

Emma stared down at her. It wasn't just any Sarah; it was one of the Luddites. Their Sarah. Her eyes stared blankly up at her. She knelt down, cradled her head in her arms. "How are you here? Why are you..." She shuffled over to the man and pulled off his mask. Red-faced, red beard. It was Stuart. He guarded the island's Broch at night. He guarded them while they slept. She backed away from both bodies, her mind reeling.

"Is everything okay, Emma?" James asked.

She composed herself before nodding her head. "Aye, get on your horse. We have to leave."

"If it wasn't for your desire to torture that man, we could have left much earlier. You cost us time, even if you saved us from death."

She shook her head, the faces of her comrades still in her vision. Leaping onto her horse, she gave it a swift kick and caught up to James. "I needed time for the poison to take effect, but I didn't do all that just to avoid death, James. That was for you, too. If I lose Ned, I'm going to slit your throat, and I need you to know that I won't hesitate."

CHAPTER TWENTY-SIX

NICHOLAS WOKE to the smell of whisky. It burned through his nose far enough to reach his throat.

"Hey! -ey, liddle man, you alive?"

He propped himself up on his elbows to see a dirty fellow with a white beard speckled with black hair, or dirt. He didn't seem the sort to care either way.

"Oh, yer alive? Yer alive, right?" He hiccupped.

"Aye, I'm alive," Nicholas responded through a faint pounding at his temples.

"Well, tha's gud. Some o' 'em other folks were lookin' to steal yer money, but I says to 'em, 'No! We dunnae even know if he's dead yet.'"

"Thanks for that."

"No' a problem. Besides, I already checked and ye had none." The man laughed with a wheeze of equal parts alcohol, blood, and rotting teeth. After imparting that bit of truth, he stumbled away to High Street.

The rider and horse were gone; the fog receded, as well.

Parents blew out candles in the surrounding flats, putting children to bed. What time is it?

Something tugged on his neck. A key on a worn silver chain. He held it to the light of the torches lit in the square. The fire danced against the silver and played in the tiny etchings on its surface. A series of letters and numbers.

M.C. -273

Makar's Court? Nicholas hadn't seen a house number like this, though.

The homes in Makar's Court were stone and wooden patchwork, nothing special. The court had only two exits. At the far end, a small staircase led to nothing, a former door long since covered. He climbed it anyway to get a better view of the space. Light from the torches threw deep shadows across the stonework, casting even small objects as monstrous. He couldn't spot the number anywhere.

Look below.

Across the square, in front of one of the building entrances, the light bounced golden off what looked like a plaque set in the ground. How had he missed this? A strange sensation crept up on him the closer he came to it. It wasn't excitement or mere curiosity, it was more like an old habit, as if he'd done this before or would do it many times in the future.

He kneeled down to read the engraving. It was small, free of flourish.

Makar's Court
Negative Two Hundred and Seventy-Three

The words were stamped into a plate with a tiny keyhole

punched into it. He ran his finger around the edge. A chill ran up his arm.

He took the key from his neck, slid it into the lock, and turned. He heard a familiar click and then an unfamiliar grinding of metal. Not loud, but something set in motion under the stones. The grinding gave way to a soothing ticking of gears spinning into place, followed, at last, by an exhale of steam. Four puffs of warm mist sprayed through invisible holes between the rocks. The condensed air revealed a rectangular cut in the stonework, distinguishing the rock of the court from the rock of an entrance. Nicholas placed his hand on the counterfeit section and pushed. It gave way; the ticking of another set of gears spun as a passage underground revealed itself.

Had no one else seen this before? He worried about someone trying to follow him, but all the lights in the windows were out.

Biting air emanated from the hole, but yellow light beamed from somewhere deeper. At any rate, it looked more inviting than spending the night on the darkening streets of Edinburgh. The sound of breaking glass rang through the close to reinforce this thought.

Nicholas put the key back around his neck, cast a look to the sky, and descended a steel staircase.

The passageway was well lit, but freezing. He stuffed his hands into his pockets. Metal plates lined the walls of the hall, much of it rusted in the corners where the plating met, and moisture collected. A red pipe ran along the length of both sides of the passage before disappearing around a corner further down. At regular intervals, the pipe fed into glass orbs, each one filled with a glowing amber mist. He saw no flame of any kind. The swirling air itself seemed to produce the light. If the promise of more mystery wasn't beckoning, he might have stayed to watch it longer.

He noted that it was well looked after, despite the small amount of rust. Nicholas steeled himself against the thought of someone else being down here. He had his fill of mysterious strangers.

He rounded the corner into a circular room filled with machinations of all kinds, all inactive. Some appeared to function independently of others, while many looked interlocked. Nicholas couldn't tell where one started, and another ended. It could have been one massive device for all he knew. Gears and flasks and steel tubes attached to rods of a second metal, hoses, chains, buckles, and straps decorated the room, fulfilling some unknown purpose. If it all belonged to a single machine, he'd seen nothing like it.

It was warmer in this room. A large table made from a black wood, gnarled legs, sat in the middle of the room. It was clean save for a brass object with an emerald-green top and a second plaque like the one outside.

Wary of the dormant instrument springing to life, he stepped towards the desk, keeping a watchful eye on the metal mass.

As he got closer, he discovered the plaque to be blank. He rubbed his fingers across its surface and felt tiny bumps graze his fingertips. A chain hung from the brass item and Nicholas saw no reason to not pull it, so he did. Light spilled across the desk, and the etching came into view. It was some sort of lantern. He pulled the drawstring again, and the light went away, along with the words. He pulled it a third time and there it was, clear as anything else in the room. Nicholas amused himself a few more times with the illusion before reading the message.

You are everywhere and nowhere.
May you find the tools you need to live up to your name.

He felt like a burglar. This message couldn't be for him, but then why did he end up with the key? His thoughts bounced from one question to another, one conclusion to another.

Nicholas looked back through the tunnel. He couldn't go home at this hour.

The great apparatus loomed over him like Edinburgh Castle did the city above. Three red wooden knobs protruded from its centre. He already knew he wouldn't last the night without turning at least one. The knobs were in a vertical sequence, so he thought it best to use the first one. He curled his fingers around it, took a deep breath in, and with a good amount of force, turned it.

He got a response. Quiet at first, like the bubbling of hot water for tea, then a hiss spurred events into action. Steam shot from several holes in tubing and rods. Pistons started a march in clockwise rotation. Several steel buckles fastened to a fabric sack snapped open to allow it to expand.

Nicholas stepped back behind the desk, half expecting the machine to bulge and burst. After much commotion, a small metallic arm revealed itself from a deep recess, grasping a small steel tube. It slid into place under a beaker of water and a spark igniting from inside it produced a tiny blue flame. The surrounding air rippled.

Within moments, the water boiled, producing huge plumes of steam that flushed into a connected cylinder, putting an enormous amount of pressure on a quantity of amber gas. As the steam grew more and more opaque, the golden light grew brighter, vibrating as it did.

Something released behind the walls and the now-familiar sound of scraping metal arose to Nicholas's left. One of the wall panels fell back until it lay parallel to the floor. Chains on either side pulled the panel upwards into the ceiling, giving Nicholas a clear view of the room beyond.

Then everything went quiet. The machine shut down with only a hiss of steam and a few clinks as mechanisms found their original homes again.

He peered into the new room and what he saw was something so mundane, so unexpected, he almost found it harder to believe than what he had just witnessed. It was a bedroom.

A luxurious bed piled high with red blankets and pillows dominated the small room. In the corner, a large armoire stood, fashioned from the same black wood as the desk. It matched a small table beside the bed that supported several tiny brass objects strewn across its top. Some of them were in disrepair. A spring or a small gear lay about, along with a few tools suited for small pieces. Leaning against one wall was a large bookcase bursting with old tomes and yellowed papers, some tattered, others burned at the edges.

Suddenly filled with mischief, Nicholas darted back to the other two knobs and turned them both before he could reconsider. The machine groaned to life once again, this time with considerable effort and enough of a racket that Nicholas feared it might attract attention above ground.

After a similar production, a second room revealed itself. He expected a third, but found only disappointment when, instead, a small panel opened nearby. Inside, a vial filled with amber liquid, so bright it was difficult to look at, hung suspended over a golden crystal. The gem pulsed, but it wasn't hot. Nicholas held his hand close to it, to be sure. It was in a deep recess and the constant throb of light reminded Nicholas of a beating heart. His eyes widened. This must be what makes it work. The liquid in the vial hanging above it wasn't boiling or swirling around like it was elsewhere in the room. It didn't seem to be responding to anything. Even a tap on the side of the glass had no effect. A small dial above the panel ticked away, but not in any interval Nicholas recognized. He tried to time the dial's movements by counting seconds on his fingers, but it never matched up. The delay between ticks wasn't even uniform. The dial moved in less than a second and then, at other moments, took several.

Shrugging his shoulders, he left the mystery behind to enter the new room. It was larger than the bedroom, with black shelving around the perimeter, all home to hundreds, thousands, of tiny compartments, each one holding a secret.

In the centre of the room stood a circular table, black to match the rest of the furnishings. It wasn't a complete circle, though. An inlet at the far end would allow Nicholas to stand in the middle.

He pulled open a few of the compartments along the outer wall. One held screws; another held a selection of tiny gears like the ones in the bedroom. Still others with glass tubes and scraps of cloth. There were buttons and thread, aromatic spices, lock picks, rivets, and nails.

Whoever lived here was a craftsman.

After looking at all the compartments he'd opened, he let out a deep yawn. He looked back through the entrance to see the bedroom not far beyond. Since the key hung around his neck, he wagered it would be all right to sleep here for at least one night.

Despite everything, he couldn't push the image of his parents from his mind, even with the constant barrage of fantastic events. He hung his coat on one bedpost, his hand lingered on the fabric before letting it go.

He threw several of the pillows off the bed until finding one that suited him. It was firm and cool on his cheek. The blankets were heavy and pulled him into the bedding underneath. The ever-present amber light would make sleeping a little more difficult, so he turned away from it and closed his eyes.

Deep in his mind, in the very pit of it, the thought stirred that he was not here at all. That he was back in his hamlet, waiting to wake to relive the trauma of that morning again. He gripped the edge of the pillow hard, hoping it would be enough to keep him in this spot throughout the night.

CHAPTER TWENTY-SEVEN

THE BEATING of hooves sparked wildfires inside Ned's skull. White light overwhelmed his senses and made it too difficult to tell where the bounty hunters were taking him. He snapped several branches when the horse rode a little too close to the side of the road. They were clean, solid breaks. Emma would spot them.

After an hour's ride, the sky split, and rain beat down on them with intention. Ned shivered, soaked through. The rider he clung to threw his cape around them both. A live prisoner is worth more than a dead one. But he worried more that the storm would wash away their trail. More than likely, this is why the bounty hunters risked sticking to the main roads. Ned hoped his own markers would be enough.

The group halted. The riders exchanged muffled words, before he heard a few of them break off from the group and carry on down the road.

"Where are we going?" Ned asked.

"We're making camp for the night," the rider replied.

"Where are the others going?"

"They'll keep riding for a while before circling back at a split in the road. Precautions. In case anyone follows us, or if that woman with you takes down Stu—"

"No names!" barked another.

"Ach, it doesn't matter what he knows. He'll be with us another day and then him and all his sorry followers will be someone else's problem," the rider shouted back.

"What if she finds you before then?" Ned asked.

"Who? That lady with you? Goodness, she looked good with a knife, but Stu'll break her in two. He gets a thrill from beating on women, I think."

"Especially when they fight back," another said, laughing.

"Aye. Doesn't matter though. There's no reward for your bitch. So, either she dies there or dies here. It makes no difference to my coin purse."

The lead rider whistled, and the four horses tightened formation as they made their way through the dense trees of Hill Wood. Ned snapped as many branches as he could on the way into the foliage.

A short distance from the road, the group found a small clearing and tied the horses up.

"Get off," his companion gruffed.

"I can't see," Ned said.

"Ach, it's not that dark. Get off the horse."

"No, I mean I cannot see. I'm blind. I'll need help off the horse," Ned said.

"What are you on about?" the rider asked. "Hey, did you know he's blind?" he shouted to one of the others.

He could hear a pair of them approach the horse. "Look at me."

Ned turned towards the voice.

"A blind man leading a bunch of fools. It's no wonder you're all gettin' hanged." The group laughed. "What a joke."

"You sure this is even him?" another asked.

"Aye, it's him. Looks like the poster, 'cept for all them ladies' underwear."

"You like dressin' up like a woman? Filth."

Then a hand gripped Ned's shoulder and pulled him off the horse. His world flipped upside-down, and he landed in the mud with a smack. A small rock dug into his shoulder. More laughter from the group.

"Don't kill 'im. We want as much of the reward as possible."

"I ain't gonna kill 'im. I think he's puttin' up a fight, though. A small beatin' might set him straight. Somethin' ain't right with a man who wears a lady's undergarments."

That's when the kicking started. The rain still threw his new sense off, making it impossible for him to see where they were coming from. His leather took the brunt of the blows, but not completely. He rolled onto his stomach before rising to his knees, his hands raised to deflect the blows.

He misjudged the hunters' capacity for pity and felt large solid knuckles across his cheek. His entire body launched into the ground. Coppery blood filled his mouth, as did mud.

"Bloody molly can't even defend himself! How the fuck is this buggerer leadin' an army?"

"From the rear, is my guess!" More cackling.

Another fist slammed into the back of his head. It drove his nose into the sludge, his lungs filled with muck. He gasped for air; his insides pressed against his already bruising ribs.

"Enough. You're hitting a blind man, you sacks o' shite." One of the voices said above the chaos.

He rolled over and his sight flooded with white as another fist slammed down on him. He felt something crunch in his face as the blow landed. His cheek split open and warm blood mixed with cool water as it poured from his face. The men kept laughing.

"Blind or no, he got my brother-in-law, a proper soldier, killed in a factory fire his lot started. I ain't gonna let that go. We'll get our reward, and this waste of flesh will show up at the courts as black and blue as he leaves his men's asses after he fucks 'em. You have a problem wi'that then take your merry bit and go build us a fire until we're done 'ere."

"Please, stop. We don't kill anyone. We've never killed—," Ned called out, but his voice caught in his throat.

They took turns now. One would kick, another punched. They hurled insults at him. He didn't feel it anymore. Adrenaline numbed him, each strike duller than the last, like the blunt end of an axe against the bark of a tree. No bite, but there would be if he lasted until morning.

Hate them.

The rain stopped. His body and face warmed. He didn't hear the men anymore. In fact, he heard nothing. No horses, no wind, no leaves rustling. He uncurled and searched for something to pull himself up. His hand swung through the air before he let it fall to the ground, but even then, it fell through that, as well. He wasn't in contact with anything. He was in mid-air. Not falling, but floating.

"Hello?" he muttered, blood filling the cracks in his lips. He kicked his legs out. Still nothing.

The sensation lasted only a few moments before the world came rushing back to him with a distant scream cut short.

Several tiny pinpoints of light broke his dark surroundings. Then the rain returned and splashed against his broken face. The blurred edges of treetops lined his peripheral, the pinpoints of light revealing themselves as stars. The rest of the world came into view as he sat up, and winced as he did, wounds already settling in.

He could see again.

He flinched when he saw the silhouettes of the men still surrounding him, but they didn't advance. Pulling himself to his feet, he leaned on a nearby crate for support. The men weren't moving, their bodies rigid.

"Tired of beating on a blind man?" Ned shouted.

His vision sharpened and adrenaline urged him forward. They were too still.

"Hello?"

As he limped towards them, moonlight cut through the clouds and cast everything in a silver pale. All three were dead, their insides exposed to the air. Carved, sliced at bizarre angles. The one closest to Ned was almost completely gone. His face cut back to reveal only the back half of his brain, the front missing. Half of his stomach, his lungs, most of his heart, gone. He stood like a human shelf, his organs on display like museum curios, bones sliced open, yellow marrow glistening like oil. Two of them were in the same state, but the one furthest away kept more of his face, anger still visible in the expression around his eyes.

Rain picked up, the heavy drops eroding the bodies bit by bit.

Ned's stomach clenched, and he vomited. The contents mixed with the blood and rainwater in his mouth. That's when he noticed the pit around him. The ground cratered, scooped out in the same circular fashion. He stood at the centre of a sphere of carnage.

Water pooled around his feet, washing away the evidence, if not the memory, of the slaughter.

CHAPTER TWENTY-EIGHT

NICHOLAS DID, in fact, wake in the same place as he went to sleep the night before. The only thing that changed was the neatness of his hair and the pile of blankets and pillows kicked to the floor. His eyes opened first, with no other movement from his body. He heard ticking and half-wondered if some giant metal beast had come to feed on him for sleeping in its bed.

Once he sat up and looked around the room, he saw no such machination. A tiny orb, filled with the familiar glowing steam, sprung to life on the bedside table. Nicholas rolled across the bed and snatched the sphere from its pedestal. Gold trim bisected the gadget. It continued to tick, the top hemisphere turning independently of the bottom.

Nicholas placed the marble back on the stand and waited to see what would happen, each tick bringing him closer to revealing another mystery.

It clicked into its last position, and a sharp note, like a whistle, rang out. It was shrill enough to make Nicholas wince. From an unseen hole in its top, a blast of wet mist sprayed out from inside. The vapour settled across the head of the bed, wetting the only remaining pillow. The halves then fell apart, clanking against the table, and spilling their secrets in the form of a slip of paper.

Nicholas glanced at the soggy pillow, confused. He reached for the tiny slip of parchment and unrolled it. It read:

It is now seven o'clock in the morning.
Your breakfast is served at your desk, as usual.
Please replace this note and reset the clock before leaving.

"A clock?" Nicholas said aloud. He replaced the note inside the two halves and pushed them together. There was a satisfying click when they aligned. He spun the device back until it wouldn't go any further and repositioned it on the stand. If breakfast hadn't been mentioned, he might have been more curious.

He pulled himself from the bed and stood and, for the first time in months, the act wasn't accompanied by any pain. His knees didn't crack, his muscles didn't spasm. Not even the excitement of new discoveries could cause him to miss that fact. He jumped. Small at first, then from the bed to the floor. No pain. Curious, he thought.

His stomach growled and he remembered the promise of food.

On the table in the main room sat a bowl of oatmeal, heat still rising from it. Beside it, in a tin cup, was a fresh glass of orange juice. Nicholas paused before grabbing the spoon that lay beside the bowl. It was plain and wooden. He scooped up some of the oatmeal and touched it to his tongue. Hot, but he could taste the oats, the added lavender, and the sweetness of berries; that was good enough for his palate. Nicholas devoured the entire bowl and washed it down with the orange juice.

He wiped his mouth clean with his sleeve and looked around the room, feeling almost lost without some sort of mechanical device prompting his next move. He checked the bright vial from the night before, only to discover it was gone. Not just the contents, but the flask, too. Did it disappear back inside the machine? It must have. He continued on to the workshop, disappointed he might never learn its purpose.

Nicholas wanted to find something worthwhile in one of the hundreds of compartments yet to be opened. He checked a few of them, but found only strips of copper, tiny metallic tubes, and rubber stoppers. So, he placed a handful of items on the circular worktable, hoping he might find a use for them. Nicholas entered the inlet of the table, giving him a good view of everything he selected—a long, thin tube made of wood, a rubber stopper, a curved piece of silver metal, and a small cylinder filled with amber steam.

Some objects were foreign to him, but somehow familiar, like finding your own baby clothes.

He scooped up the small cylinder and at once the other components vibrated, their physical boundaries shifting, edges blurring. His hand felt tugged towards the rest of the pieces. Nicholas rubbed his eyes, but the components before him continued to make suggestions, connections formed like tiny rivers in the canals of his mind. Similar to the experience with the loom only days earlier, but instead of deconstructing, these objects were trying to assemble, to form something beyond his knowledge.

The glass tube slid inside the wooden cylinder, and he plugged it with the rubber stopper to keep the tube in place. He attached the final piece, the curved bit of silver metal, to a notch on the other side of the wooden cylinder, where it fixed to the wood.

Nicholas held the finished piece out in front of him. A spoon, of sorts. The metal was flat, missing the bowl shape that would make it useful.

He tested it by popping it into his mouth and the heat from his tongue softened the metal, as if it had been resting by a fire. When he pulled it from his mouth, a shallow depression had been formed.

Nicholas dropped the spoon. Did he make that?

He ran back to the shelves, spilling their contents onto the table before going back for more. Bracing himself with a hand on each side of the inlet, he surveyed the mess of parts, and waited for the objects to vibrate.

"Come on. Do it again!" he shouted.

The lamps around the room buzzed. He didn't know if it was new, or he hadn't noticed. Either way, the sound rooted itself in his ears, burrowed deeper until the hum buried itself deep inside his mind. He ran his fingertips along the bony curves under his hair. He couldn't scratch it, couldn't get rid of the sensation.

The faint scent of burning reached him, followed by the sharp crack of a whip, the splitting of an invisible tree trunk. All at once, something inside of Nicholas shifted, like the two halves of his brain coming apart, loosening, and now separating, freeing his mind from his body. His movements were methodical, calculated, and fast. Very fast.

The room twirled around him, passing in a blur. His arms felt light but purposeful.

Then, all at once, it stopped. He panted, buckled over. He did not know how much time had passed.

"Whoa."

Twenty new creations lay on the desk now. Some as simple as his spoon, others much more elaborate, their purpose unknown. He noticed a few more kitchen utensils, as well as another globe, like the one in the bedroom.

In the sudden stillness, he hesitated to reach for any of the items. Half out of fear, half out of excitement. The buzz in his skull dissipated. He pushed through his fear and picked up a copper spring missed in his frenzy, looked around the room at the myriad of unopened drawers, and smiled.

"I have to show Sam."

CHAPTER TWENTY-NINE

"NED!"

He opened his eyes. Over the treeline, the sun crested yellow, adding a buttery richness to the gore. The men still stood around the hole, their gruesome bodies now husks, the rain washing away whatever organs were still inside.

"Ned!" It was Emma's voice.

He didn't want her to see this, but he couldn't move fast enough to draw her elsewhere.

She burst through the edge of the clearing and froze. The look on her face was one Ned hadn't seen before: shock.

"What... happened?"

"I don't know."

She helped him to his feet.

"Ned, what happened to them?" she repeated.

"They were beating me. Then I felt like I was floating and then they... were like that."

James crashed through the trees next. "My god," he whispered.

"Help me get him on a horse," she said.

James wrapped Ned's arm around his neck and walked him to

one of the horses. With a pained groan, Ned pulled himself up and into the saddle.

Emma put her hand under his chin and raised his head to the light. "Ned, your face. I'm..."

He winced, and it hurt to wince.

"Feels like every part of me is broken. Most of it, anyway."

"I'm so sorry, Ned. I shouldn't have let you go."

"We'd be dead if you hadn't. What happened to the man they left behind—"

"He's dead," Emma said.

"Like them?"

"No, regular dead."

"How?"

"Me. Ned, there's something else—"

"There were others sent ahead to throw you off the trail."

"Aye, they fled. They must have seen this and ran. We need to talk—"

"What do we do? What did I do to them, Emma?" Ned asked. As if they were new to him, he stared into his hands.

"Don't speak. Just rest."

"We need to get him back to the city, to a doctor," James said.

"You need to shut your mouth before I cut it open from ear to ear. No more words from you. You've brought nothing but misery into his life. Ned would be leading a raid right now if it wasn't for you. Instead, he's been struck blind and beaten nearly to death and —" she choked on her words and turned away from both James and Ned for a moment, "and something is happening to him I can't explain. So, if you have nothing left to offer us, then you should leave now while I still have the sense to let you."

"Emma, it's not his fault," Ned said.

"It is his fault! It's his fault for leading us here, and it's my fault for convincing you to follow him."

"Emma, this is not your fault, either."

"I'm supposed to protect you, Ned. I'm supposed to save you from all of this, and I keep failing."

Ned propped himself up on his horse. "You have never failed me, Emma."

"Ned, Emma, please."

"I told you to shut your mouth, James!" Emma drew a small sword from a pack on her horse and held it against his throat.

James raised his hands. "If you kill me, you'll never know what's happening to him," he pleaded.

"You best speak fast. Do you know what's happening to him?"

James swallowed, his Adam's apple pushing against the tip of the sword. "I do, because it happened to me."

CHAPTER THIRTY

NICHOLAS KNEW three things about his friend Sam: she didn't stay in one place for long, she always got into places she didn't belong, and she liked turquoise. One of these facts wasn't helpful, but if she was wearing dresses to work, she might be on Princes Street.

Sam often dragged Nicholas up and down the area, pressing her filthy fingers against the glass of any shop window with an extravagant dress fitted to a mannequin inside. The more opulent the dress, the longer she lingered. She would never want to wear them, as she expressed on repeated occasions. She only ever wanted to make them. Nicholas never believed her.

She would point out quality stitching and use words she'd picked up from passersby, like *ex-quis-ite,* sounding each syllable out as if tasting each part. Half the time she wouldn't even know what they meant, but Nicholas nodded along.

Princes Street was part of New Town. Nicholas preferred the style of buildings in Old Town, but he did like some niceties of the newer area. There was an order to the way the streets aligned that differed from the branching, curving streets that wound their way through Old Town. New Town conquered the land; Old Town moulded itself to it.

The Earthen Mound connected Old Town to New Town, a land bridge stretching across the entire North Loc. What was once a perilous expanse was now filled with rubbish and soil from the new homes built in New Town. Edinburgh lost a quarry ripe for mischief and gained a tiresome land bridge, much to their disappointment.

Nicholas trekked across the mound, which always took longer than he thought it would. Unfortunately, the pain in his legs had returned. His feet sunk into the damp earth, his shoes becoming filthier with each step. The city made earlier attempts to construct a few smaller buildings on the mound, but nothing substantial. The men at the coal mine mentioned that some merchants were looking to start a bank in the area. Nicholas's family had little use for one of those.

The mound deposited him along Princes Street, where shops lining both sides of his route displayed what the wealthy were wearing. One shop, for men's clothing, housed a green waistcoat with gleaming golden buttons dotting its front. He looked at the cuff of his own jacket. The threads were loose, the edges stained white from sweat.

A few carriages turned down the street in the distance, leaving behind them the scent of horse dung. Other than two beadsmen on their way to St. Giles Cathedral, he was alone, which, at the very least, would make it easier to spot Sam.

The emptiness increased the scale of the city, though. He'd only ever been to a few locations before and therefore Edinburgh always felt more like a series of small rooms and not the unexplored expanse he found himself in. He felt insignificant. Having spent the night under it made him realise there was no real chance of finding Sam. She might even be at home.

He sighed and slumped against the nearby window, stuffing his hands in his pockets. The scent of rich meat pie overtook his sense of defeat and pulled him back onto the street. The aroma filled the lane and made his stomach growl.

He scanned his options, of which there were plenty. He settled on the one closest when something pricked his mind.

No, the next one.

The voice returned, and with it a headache he needed to sit down for. He recognized it now as the man on the white horse. Nicholas looked for him, but he knew he would not see him. Whatever was happening was happening inside his own mind. He didn't have to listen to it, but if he hadn't followed the man, he would never have found the workshop. So, Nicholas would play along for a bit longer. Mr. Morgan's Butchery it is, then.

He found a table inside and took a seat. He waited until the butcher, bringing a suckling pig from the back, noticed him.

"What are you doin' there? You eatin'?" the butcher asked.

Nicholas nodded. "Just a pie, sir."

"You got the coin?"

Nicholas pulled a few from his pocket. The display sufficed, and the butcher set to work plating one of his steaming pies for his young customer.

It arrived, hot and golden. His stomach murmured again, but he didn't manage a single bite before the door swung open. A well-dressed man stepped inside. He wore a peculiar pair of black, round-framed glasses that matched the colour of his pointed beard. A green top hat with silver trim caught Nicholas's eye. The man removed it from his head, revealing a shiny scalp void of hair. He tucked the hat under his arm and took several smooth strides to the butcher's counter. He looked like he wanted to place an order, then turned back to the open doorway.

"Samantha, come along," the man said.

Nicholas heard small footsteps on the stones leading into the shop. Then, as if conjured by his own will, Sam entered. Or at least someone who resembled her. The girl wore a dress finer than he'd ever seen, purple, like heather. Her shoes sparkled, hair pulled back in white ribbons, and powder covered her face.

"I'm sorry for taking so long," she said.

"You apologise. You are indeed sorry, but you offer your apologies," he said to her, squeezing her by the wrist.

At first, Nicholas wasn't sure it was Sam, but her boyish mannerisms soon broke through her awkward attempts at pageantry. Nicholas still saw his friend in all that disguise. The well-dressed man ordered, and Nicholas saw his chance. He sidled up beside her and said, "Hi."

Sam did a double take. Her eyes grew wide, and she gasped. Her cheeks flushed even more than the rouge insinuated.

"Nico?" she whispered.

He smiled at her, thankful to see a friendly face.

"What are you doing here?" she whispered.

"Eating meat pie," he said, pointing to his table. "Want me to get you one?" he asked.

"No, I'm working, Nico. I can't eat right now."

"Can you meet me later?"

"No, go away."

"Why?"

"I'm working."

"I know, but I want to show you something incredible!"

Her lower jaw pushed forward. She always did that when he annoyed her.

"Okay, okay, meet me at Makar's Court at midnight. I'll wait for you," he said.

The well-dressed man turned to make a note of Nicholas, then glared down at Sam.

"Samantha, don't talk to those in lower stations," he said in an even tone, as if he wasn't being offensive, rather stating the obvious.

"My apologies," she said in a sweet voice laced with more formality than she'd ever spoken with before.

Nicholas returned to his table, confused.

"Let's be on our way then," the man said, having concluded his business. He extended an arm to Sam, who took it with grace. It unsettled Nicholas to see them like that. Sam flashed him a fiery stare as they turned to leave.

"Bye, Sam," he said.

The well-dressed man turned to Nicholas. He towered over him.

"How dare you address my companion."

Nicholas stammered at first, then Sam's expression told him not to speak.

The man exchanged a glance with Samantha. He raised his cane and stuck it into the middle of Nicholas's meat pie. "If you see her again, you'll walk the other way. Are you able to understand me?"

Nicholas did not respond.

The man swiped his cane to the side and sent the pie and its metal dish crashing to the floor.

The butcher stepped out. "Hey, leave that boy alone. Get along now."

The well-dressed man flashed a yellow smile at Nicholas. "Filth protects filth." He then wiped the gravy that stuck to his cane on the arm of Nicholas's jacket.

Nicholas smacked it to the side, and it came loose from the man's grasp. He stood up and, surprising himself, took an aggressive stance in front of the well-dressed man.

"Try that again and I'll shove that cane up yer arse so far you'll be the first to taste Mr. Morgan's meat pie from the other direction."

Sam gasped.

"Samantha, retrieve my cane," the man said.

"Oh, don't trouble the lady," he mocked. "I'll get your bloody cane."

But the man placed a hand on Nicholas's chest. "I insist. Samantha, retrieve it."

Samantha made her way through the tables and chairs to the rod and brought it back to the well-dressed man, who didn't break his gaze at Nicholas. She polished the decorative ornament, a sprig of holly, with a handkerchief.

"Thank you," he said.

Then he struck her across the face, sending her into one of the tables.

Nicholas lunged at the man but met the polished end of the cane with the side of his head, dizzying him.

Mr. Morgan came rushing out from behind the counter, but with a sharp turn of his heels, the well-dressed man grabbed Samantha by the arm and dragged her, stumbling, out and into a carriage.

Mr. Morgan shuffled towards Nicholas. "Stay still. You took a right good knock on the head."

"I need to get after her," he muttered.

"Do you know who that man is, lad?" Mr. Morgan asked.

He shook his head.

"Slow down. Catch your breath. Don't find yourself muddled in that man's business. He makes trips to Edinburgh a few times a year, he does. Terrible things I've heard. Folks call him the Dollmaker," he said.

"The doll maker? He makes toys?" Nicholas asked.

"Not quite, lad. Look, if your friend is with him, she's in trouble. No lass would take up with 'im by choice."

CHAPTER THIRTY-ONE

EMMA PUSHED the tip of her sword as deep as she could into James's throat without piercing it. A small bead of blood formed at the point and ran down the front of the blade.

"You knew what was happening, but didn't share it? That's what you think will save you from me?" she asked.

"Please, let me explain."

"Emma, wait. Hear him out," Ned said.

Emma withdrew her sword. Instead, she swatted the back of his legs with the flat side of the blade, forcing him to his knees. "Talk. Now."

"These things that are happening to you. It's who you are. You're like me, like my father and his father before him. We have gifts. I'm not sure why yours have only manifested now, but when we met, I knew immediately that you didn't know. I thought to trigger them by putting you in touch with people from your past or by putting you in stressful situations."

"Excellent. Can I kill him now?" Emma asked.

"James, you need to do a lot better or I won't be able to stop her."

"This is the best way." James's eyes followed Emma as she walked circles around him. "I know it's a lot to hear, but I knew if you experienced them first, it would be easier to believe me. The merchant, you met him as a child. I'm not sure why you don't remember, but you met him. He was present during a meaningful moment in your life. Do you not remember?"

"I don't, James. I never remember anything. Nothing you've told me has brought back a single memory. So, what was it? Did he sell us potatoes? Bring us a ham?"

"No, Ned. You were with him when your mother died."

Ned's head fell to his chest. "I'm sorry. I wish I could remember. I wish I could remember her."

"Me too."

Emma stepped between them. "No, none of this makes sense. You don't remember any of this and he's filling in your memories with lies. You don't know if any of this is—"

"Emma! If there's a chance it's not true, then there's also a chance it is true. I'll err on trust every time."

"You're a damn fool," Emma said.

"Ned, I'm drawn to these people, the ones who trigger these reactions in you. I can feel them pulling at me and it's working, just not as expected. It may be that because you didn't grow up with these gifts, they're overwhelming you. Your second sight, the one made of light, connects to time itself. In its infancy, it allows you to see a few seconds or minutes ahead."

"How do you know that?" Emma asked.

"My father had the same gift. And the men back in the clearing, they beat you?"

"Aye."

"You were angry and scared?"

Ned nodded.

"Your desperation released a gift I wasn't aware you had. This may be difficult to explain. You can move great distances in an instant. You alone, your physical body, can slip through a window and appear wherever you want. However, because you can't control it, the window grew beyond your body in what looks like a spherical shape that took pieces of whatever it touched with it."

"You're saying I killed those men? I did that to them?"

James nodded. "Not intentionally, but yes."

"This is madness. I can't believe we're entertaining this," Emma said.

"Is it, Emma?" James asked.

"Yes, it is."

"Have you not seen this happen before?"

Emma froze. She abandoned her pacing and stared at James.

"What's he talking about?" Ned asked.

"I have tricks of my own. Nothing like Ned, but we come from the same line. I know what you saw in the alley. Tell us."

"How did you—"

"I sense things. Thoughts, actions, when they're strong enough, I sometimes see them play out in front of me."

"You have no right—" Emma said.

"You have no right keeping it from him. He did this once already, and you knew it."

"Emma?"

She looked at him, her face pained. He could tell she didn't want to speak, but he had to know.

"What is he talking about?"

She breathed out a long breath, delaying it as long as she could. "I found Mr. Chapman further down the same alley we found you, his body was sliced open just like these men. I wanted to tell you, but you were already dealing with so much and I did not know it… was you that caused it."

"Well, it appears no one is being completely honest with you, Ned."

Emma turned and kicked James square in the chest. He buckled over, gasping for air.

"Shut your mouth, you snake," Emma spat.

"Emma, take a breath. Go for a walk."

She shook her head and stomped off into the trees.

Through intermittent coughing, James said, "Ned, you're meant for something great, and we must continue the path set out for you if you're to be restored. Don't let her stop you. She'll never understand," he wheezed, "what you and I understand."

Ned kneeled in front of James. "Where does this path lead next?" Ned asked.

James rolled over and back to his knees. "Inverness."

Ned placed his hand on his shoulder. "Who am I to meet there?"

"An old friend."

"An old friend? I have no old friends, James. In fact, I have only one friend. I trust her in every way. If she withheld something from me, it's because it was necessary to do so. I believe you've spoken the truth just now, but I also know you dole it out piecemeal when you see fit for your purposes, for your ends. You have manipulated me from the start. That type of person is worse than a liar and I regret finding that quality in a man who may be my father. She is a better friend than you will ever be."

Ned moved his hand from James's shoulder to his throat and drove him up against a tree trunk.

"And if you ever try to divide us again, I will end your life. The only reason I allow you to stay with us is because of whatever small slivers of truth you might still hold back from me. If I were you, I would hang onto those. You'll need them."

He released James, who broke into a coughing fit again.

Emma returned, and Ned motioned her over.

"What happened to him?" she asked.

"You kicked him pretty hard," Ned said, smiling. He breathed in deep and winced before whispering, "I understand how ridiculous this sounds, but I believe him."

"Do you believe him because he's right, or because you want him to be right?" Emma asked.

"What do you mean?" Ned asked.

"I've never met a man who would turn down the chance to be a god, Ned. Most of you think you already are one. Surely there's a more rational explanation for what's happening. Transportive windows? Travelling through time? This is absurd."

"It is, but can you explain it any other way?"

"I can't, but that doesn't make it true."

"Aye, well said."

"We return to the island," he paused, making sure James could hear, "with James. Bound."

Emma jerked the old man to his feet and pushed him towards her horse. "Not quite what I hoped for, but I'll still make you as uncomfortable as possible," Emma said.

She pulled a short length of rope from her saddlebag and tied it around James's wrists, squeezing them together so that the skin went white in places. James grunted but did not put up a fight.

"One more thing," Emma said, before moving in closer to Ned. "Did you get a look at any of the bounty hunters? Any of them take their masks off?"

"No, I was blind until I..."

"The two they left behind with me, it was Sarah and Stuart. They might have all been Luddites."

Ned stared at her, confused. "What? No, they wouldn't do that. I trained Sarah myself."

"I didn't want to believe it either, but there are desperate people in that lot. The promise of a reward might've been too tempting. It was strange, though. Stuart didn't make any indication that he knew me. I can't explain it."

"There were only a handful of them, though. That means the rest of the Luddites will strike the factory in New Lanark tonight, just as we planned. They wouldn't delay because of my absence. We need to gather them. Sticking together is the best option. Stop the raids, return with the spring when the bounty has cooled."

James, overhearing bits and pieces of their conversation, said, "Ned, we must not miss our meeting in Inverness."

"I won't be taking your council on where I must and must not be. If the meeting is of enough importance, it will wait. If it does not, you and I will part ways and never speak again. Consider that a mercy."

James, dejected, slumped into Emma's horse. "I'm sorry, Ned. I knew I risked losing your trust, but I didn't think you would come with me if I told you everything at once."

"Emma, help him onto your horse."

"Can you ride?" she asked Ned.

"It's going to hurt, but I think so. Let's go find my army."

CHAPTER THIRTY-TWO

NICHOLAS RAPPED his knuckles along the cracked walls of Lady Stair's Close in time with the bell from the nearby cathedral. Twelve chimes. Sam should arrive soon.

He looked down at the key hanging from his neck before doing the same with the plaque—still there. Even seeing the key and plaque now wasn't enough to convince himself that yesterday's events happened.

Footsteps clicked towards the entrance to the close from High Street and he held his breath—not her. A stooped figure limped by, cane clicking against the cobbled street.

Nicholas resumed wearing his knuckles down to the bone for a few more minutes. He returned to the square to see if Sam had entered from a different direction, but still nothing.

He waited for a full hour before deciding she wasn't coming. Disappointed, he returned to the workshop beneath the city.

Each night for a full week, he returned topside to wait for Sam, but she never came. His disappointment grew for the first few nights, but it soon waned, and he allowed himself to get lost in his new surroundings. When he wasn't waiting or sleeping, small discoveries consumed him.

He had walked each area of the workshop multiple times, but there were still so many secrets. Did the machine change in small ways each day? How else could he explain the new levers or buttons he never noticed before? He inspected every inch of metal and still found new mysteries.

An ever-present hum weaselled its way inside his ear until he no longer noticed it. There were times he thought the workshop whispered to him or, at the very least, it breathed. It was more than just the occasional release of steam. It responded to him. He was sure of it.

After a few days, he stopped making trinkets. He grew tired of the random suggestions intruding on his thoughts. Instead, he dreamed up new ideas of his own, a growing desire to impart his will on the workshop. It all came so easily. He replicated a small toy he'd seen in the city years ago, somehow pulling the design from the recesses of his mind. He made himself a new pair of boots and a fine bag for his father, one he'd never be able to afford. Still, he was sure there was so much more the workshop had yet to reveal.

By the fifth night, he found himself speaking aloud to the machine, certain it was listening.

"I will not do what you want me to do," he said. "The key is mine. The man left it with me, so you'll listen to me now. No more spoons, no more baubles. We can do more than that," he said, tapping a finger on the glass.

No matter what he said, he was only ever met with a sigh of steam or a buzz of current.

After a full week of honing his skills, Nicholas was unsatisfied, despondent at the realization that Sam still hadn't come. He discovered something remarkable and couldn't share it with his best friend.

He left the workshop at midnight on the seventh day. He no

longer paced around the square, having resigned himself to disappointment. He tired of the ritual and turned in early. But as he unlocked the door, he heard shuffling behind him.

Pick your feet up.

His father's words flashed through his mind.

Across from him, from out of the close, a thin, tall frame stumbled towards him, red hair lit at the edges by an unseen lamp.

"Sam?"

She left the darkness of the close. It was her. The week's bitterness left him in an instant.

"Sam! You came! You will not believe this," he shouted to her.

She groaned. "You're... a... hmmmmhhhheeh... not... going to... believe," she said, her words slurred.

She muttered and made noises under her breath. Her dress, the same one she wore last he saw her, was now ruffled and soiled. The hem at the bottom frayed in places; loose blue threads reached outward from the cloth, struggling to get away.

"Sam?"

"Nico... I knew... I knew I cud, I don–," she took a sharp breath in and lifted her head.

When she looked at him, she burst out laughing. "You look... s-so strange... like a tiny man," she giggled again.

Her eyes were glassy and red; the angle of the light cast a fierce contrast of skin and shadow across her face.

"Sam, what's wrong with you?"

She stumbled then, the toe of her black shoe kicking an upturned stone. Nicholas darted forward to support her, catching her before she hit the ground, but his legs couldn't support them both and they fell to the ground together. Her head flopped backwards at an almost alarming angle; her eyes stared into his. The smell of stale whisky poured from her mouth.

He propped her up, cradling her in his arm. "You've been drinking?"

Then she emptied her stomach into the middle of Makar's Court.

The evening didn't go quite the way Nicholas expected. Without knowing what he should do, he helped Sam down into the workshop and laid her on the bed, hoping she would wake up.

The act was easier down here. As soon as he entered, he felt his strength return. He was able to put her arm over him and walk her into the bedroom without any protest from his knees. Was it the temperature? The metal? The amber gas? He didn't understand it, but he appreciated it.

Three hours passed. Her chest expanded with each breath, a silent reassurance. The timer beside him ticked away the seconds. His eyes grew heavy, but he clenched his jaw and lifted his head every time she made a noise before bringing it down once again onto the back of his hand; the tiny bones under his skin shuffling around to make room for his chin.

He glanced over at a wooden cup filled with water. There was a spout on the machine in the main room now. A tiny lever filled the cup with cold water or hot water. Unfortunately, the current situation tempered his excitement about the discovery.

Sam shivered, so he pulled the blankets up around her shoulders. Her pale hand gripped the edge of the sheet and she buried herself deep in the covers.

Nicholas walked around to the far side of the bed and lay down on top of the blankets, resting on the only unused pillow. He crossed his arms under his head and looked over at Sam. Her lips moved. It was subtle, a silent narration of whatever scene played out before her dancing eyes.

CHAPTER THIRTY-THREE

As THEY RODE over the crest of a hill that overlooked a small valley, Ned, Emma, and James saw the New Lanark cotton mill in the distance. Thick, black smoke billowed from the building. Fires inside lit windows and the entire scene glowed like a brick jack-o'-lantern. They were too late.

People who lived nearby had formed a small crowd to witness the carnage. Women and children cried. A few of the men rushed to the river, but there was nothing a bucket of water could do now. The trio slowed their horses to survey the mill, still a fair distance away.

"Well, aren't they a great lot on their own? I swear if they started that fire, I'm going to smack each one of them," Emma said.

"We don't start fires. We sabotage equipment. This mill is useless now," Ned said.

The pitch of faint shouting and the occasional crash hidden by flame and muffled by distance reached them.

They rode hard across the empty green field. The thrill of a raid washed over Ned like a sheet pulled off and over his head. He tightened his grip on the reins of his horse and kicked it hard,

adrenaline pouring into his muscles, numbing the pain of his bruises and cuts. As grass turned to stone, they rode through the village streets towards their destination, being mindful of who might watch their approach.

They stuck to the shadows and perimeters as they made their way to the rear of the mill.

A few of the Luddites there spotted him and began shouting to others of his arrival. Out of the chaos, a shadow lumbered towards them. With the fire to the figure's back, Ned couldn't see who it was until he was almost on top of him.

"Stuart!" Ned shouted. Bewildered, he glanced back at Emma.

She reached for her sword out of habit, but her face, even in low light, was riddled with confusion. Her mind was in opposition with her body, her hands fumbled, and she never drew it.

"What have you lot done?" Ned shouted.

"General, we thought you'd been captured. We moved to the next target in yer absence."

"Who ordered the fire?"

"No one, sir. We did as we always do, but—" he paused. "There are children living inside. We didn't know. They lit the fire to keep us out, but now we can't reach them. They're trapped inside, sir."

Emma grabbed him by the shoulder. "I saw you. I killed—"

Stuart was in shock, his expression bewildered.

"Where is she? Where's Sarah?" Emma demanded.

"Sarah? Her group retreated to a spot opposite the river. I ordered them to. I thought a few of us could get the children out, but the floor is already too weak."

Emma drew one of her small daggers and pushed the length along his neck. "Liar! I killed you both! You're traitors!"

Ned reached for her arm to pull it back, but in his haste, he missed and snagged the hilt of the dagger. The handle split open and a shaft of amber light poured out, lighting the area like it was the middle of the day.

A brilliant flash exploded inside Ned's mind. He saw New Lanark during the day, its looms whipping cotton in mesmerising unity. The building roared to life. Women smoking. Feet clicking on the wooden floor. A bobbin. He reached for it, and everything went dark again.

Emma stumbled back, releasing Stuart. She stood frozen, the light bending, reaching for Ned.

"What is this?" Ned asked.

"I–I don't know," she said.

"It's your dagger, Emma. What is this?"

"I know, I'm sorry, I never—"

"Thought to tell him?" James finished. "Isn't that interesting?"

As the last word left his lips, Emma threw a small knife into his arm. He screamed and slumped to his knees.

"Shut your fucking mouth, you shit!"

In one moment, she'd impaired James, returned the dagger to a position to threaten Stuart, and had drawn her sword towards Ned.

"Get away from me! All of you!" Her eyes were manic. She was in a frenzy.

Ned yelled, raising his voice above the fire, above Emma's shouts, James's cries.

Everyone froze.

"None of you move!" he yelled again. "Stuart, get the men to the river. Join up with Sarah. Head to camp as planned."

"Sir?"

"Now!"

Stuart nodded and ran off, calling to the others.

Emma's breathing was erratic. "Ned, I'm sorry. I don't know what just happened. I couldn't—" Emma asked.

"Give me that dagger."

"Ned, I—"

"Give it to me!"

Emma's jaw clenched. The light from the fire played across the muscles in her cheek. She closed the dagger's hilt and flipped the handle-end towards him. "It's yours, Ned. Always has been."

"What?"

Emma shifted uncomfortably, glancing at James.

"You and I are going to have a long talk, but we need to save those children first."

"Ned, I may be able to help," James said, grimacing through the pain.

"Are you going to deceive the fire into putting itself out?" Emma said over her shoulder.

"You might have better luck with that, my dear. Ned, I can help. I can show you how to use your gifts. Please, let me help you."

Thick black plumes of smoke boiled from the windows above, like swarms of bats pouring into the sky.

"Tell me, quick."

"Your gifts, all of them, come from a single source, a workshop. Our ancestors lived and worked and created in a place of immense power, the source of everything you can do. If you use it, even once, you'll gain the knowledge of our entire lineage."

"Faster. How will this help me now?"

"The workshop provides you with the tools you need at any moment."

Ned shook his head. "That does us no good, James. Unless the workshop is in this mill," Ned said.

"The workshop is anywhere you wish it to be, son."

"Tell me how to find it."

"Call to it. It's inside you."

"Of course. Does it have a name, then?" Emma mocked.

James ignored her. "The light inside that dagger. It entered you. It might be enough to connect you. Calm yourself, look through the flames, ignore the shouts around you and look for it. You'll know it."

The chaos around Ned was too distracting. He closed his eyes, breathed deeply, tried to ignore the persistent ache in his side, the sharp pain in his face where his flesh had been torn and beaten. The white light returned to him, and as it did, the roar of the fire heightened until he could hear nothing else. Wood popped and sizzled, then a child screamed, forcing his eyes to open.

He was no longer at the mill.

Golden light filled the room he stood in now. Shelves upon shelves stacked to the ceiling surrounded him, as did a circular table. He entered the open side and ran his calloused hands across its smooth, dark surface.

A thin rod of grey metal lay on the table. It was plain and unremarkable, especially beside the glass jar that caught his attention. A small swirl of yellow light pushed against the sides of the container, holding it captive. He held it up to his eye, shook it, and watched the intensity of the light grow for a moment before settling again.

A shiver ran up his back and he fumbled the jar. It shattered against the desk. The light left its prison like an animal testing its new boundaries, flowing with purpose. It reached towards the metal rod and covered it.

Something cold gripped his neck, his back, cradling him. His arms locked, spine ratcheted with sharp pricks up its length, then his mind emptied and soared as if beyond the boundaries of his skull. He attempted to focus on the metallic rod in front of him, but felt blind to anything he witnessed. It was a blur.

His hands burst into motion. The beast inside the machine of his mind propelled his fingers, his joints, pushing them into the metal rod. It was solid, but became malleable at his touch. For every bit that Ned shaped, the substance grew, unpacking itself. He pulled, pushed, squished, rounded, sharpened.

The amber light wrapped itself around his hands and the metal like a golden sheet. Then a flash of light, a flurry of motion, and the smoke returned to his nostrils.

"Ned! Where were you?" Emma screamed.

Ned shook his head. James leaned against a horse, nursing what looked like a fresh wound to the side of his head.

"What happened?" Ned asked.

"You left. You weren't here anymore."

"I found it. I found the workshop." Ned looked to James.

"Eventually, you'll be much quicker. So fast no one will even know you've left. If you were any longer this time, she may have finished me off," James said.

"What did I just do?" Ned asked.

"Isn't it obvious?" James nodded at Ned's hands.

Ned followed his gaze to discover he now gripped the smooth curves of a hook.

"You did exactly what you needed to."

CHAPTER THIRTY-FOUR

"NICO! NICO, WAKE UP!"

Nicholas woke to Sam's bony fingers nudging his back.

"Where are we? What is this place?"

Sam sat up in bed, the blankets tied in a bunch around her. She shook him, staring, wide-eyed, around the room.

"Stop it! I'm up! I'm up!" he said, pushing her arms away.

"Nico, where are we?" Her eyes darted back and forth, pausing on the oddities surrounding her.

He rubbed his eyes before clearing his throat. "This is what I wanted to show you."

"Then tell me where we are."

"It's a workshop. My workshop," he said, yawning, but pleased with himself. "I'll show you."

She looked at him for the first time. The remembrance of the events that led her here washed over her. "I'm so sorry. I—" her voice stopped.

"You scared me. You smelled like my uncle," Nicholas paused. "Were you drinking?"

She swallowed and her head hung downward. "They give it to

us. At work. The other girls said it would loosen me up. Maybe too much. Can we forget it?"

"Forget it? Are you—"

"Just stop asking!" Her voice raised and her head tilted towards him. "There's nothing to worry about, understand? I've been working long shifts and I'm tired and needed a good sleep. And I got one. And now I'm fine, aren't I?"

He wasn't sure if she wanted a response.

"Aren't I?"

"Aye. You seem swell now," he said, rolling his eyes.

"Good. So, where did you bring me, Nicholas Locherbie?"

He leapt from the bed, trying to shake the awkward moment as easily as she did. "It's a workshop! I met a man on a horse and I couldn't see his face and he wore a hat and he led me here and a fog rolled in around us and up the walls and he said he knew me and then I woke up and there was a key on my neck and it opened a door in the street and we're underground now and there's a machine over there that makes breakfast and steam shoots out and there's a table with a secret and another table that I can make anything I want at but I'm not great at it yet but I made some shoes and a spoon and a bag and—"

"Whoa, Nicholas. Slow down. None of that made any sense. What are you talking about?"

"Oh. Sorry."

She laughed. "Okay, who's this man on the horse?"

"I don't know. He knew me, though. He left this key with me," he said, flashing the metal around his neck. "It opened a door to this place. I've been here for a week and I, well, there are things here that I've never seen or even heard of before, Sam!"

"Like those glowing things on the wall?" she said, pointing towards the light-filled globes. "Or this metal ball that sprayed me with water?"

"Aye. I should have turned that off." He tried to hide a smile.

"Nico," she shook her head. "What have you gone and done? How did you find this place?" she asked.

"I told you, Sam. Honest. I left home, and I ended up in the market and the man on the horse—"

"With the mask and the hat,"

"Aye, the hat. And the horse was beautiful and white. He spoke to me—"

"The horse?"

"No, not the horse. The rider. I passed out, and I woke up with this key around my neck. I found a keyhole in the ground which led me down here," Nicholas said.

Sam raised her eyebrow.

"Sam, I don't know what else to say. That's what happened. It sounds mad." He let out a strong exhale, exasperated.

Sam played with a loose thread on the fringe of her dress. The room was quiet, save for the monotonous hum that Nicholas only noticed again now.

"I'm not saying this is easy to believe, Nico. I've heard you make up some good stories. You convinced Mr. Baker that his pigs ate all his chickens so you wouldn't get in trouble for letting them all escape. And I remember you stealing feathers from the butcher to throw around the pig's pen to make it look convincing," she leaned closer to him, "You're a good liar, but I also know you always tell me the truth." She slid off the bed and straightened her dress, pressing it against her legs to flatten a few of the wrinkles. "So, if this is the story you're telling me, that's the story I'll believe." She came around to his side of the bed. "Show me."

Nicholas swelled with excitement. "You're going to love this!"

She shook her head and shot him a half-smile before tugging her sleeves down over her wrists.

He led her to the main chamber, stopping only to show her the disappearing text on the table. She didn't act as excited as he was, but he knew she was hiding it. She was more impressed by the scale of the machine at the back of the room.

"What is this?" she asked, leaning in close to the glowing crystal.

"I'm not sure. I think it might be what makes it all work. The rest of it makes breakfast and opens doors, but I think it does a lot more than that. I haven't figured it out yet."

"Breakfast? I'm starving."

"In a minute. I want to show you the other room. Come, come." He pulled her into the workshop. "Okay, stand right here." Nicholas pointed to a spot just inside the door.

"What is this place?"

"See these shelves? Pick any of them. Just point."

Sam, her face scrunched up in confusion, pointed half-heartedly to a few. With each direction, Nicholas grabbed a handful of whatever he found inside. Sam picked a few he already opened and a few he hadn't.

"Okay, that should do it," he said, sorting the pieces into piles.

"What is all this stuff?" she asked.

"Screws, screw caps, a copper tube, a very tiny wooden knob, several pieces of scrap metal, some string, and a glass tube filled with the glowy stuff," he said, holding the object up for her to see.

"The glowy stuff?" she asked.

Nicholas shrugged. "It makes things work." He tapped the side of the glass cylinder and tiny yellow sparks shot out from the core.

"You're going to make something out of this?"

"I am." He moved the pieces closer together before continuing, "Oh, and I know it's going to be difficult, but I need a huge favour."

"What?"

"I need you to be quiet. It's hard enough to concentrate."

Sam rolled her eyes and leaned against the metal wall beside the door.

Nicholas waved his hand over the pieces, half trying to figure out what he should start with, half trying to play up the drama. As usual, the moment slowed as his mind came into sharp focus.

He learned more each time. It didn't feel as automatic anymore.

He understood the pieces now and didn't mash them together. The components, which he thought floated, were actually suspended by his hands. The illusion tricked him the first few times because he was moving them so fast.

Fanning out the scrap metal around the copper tube, he fastened each piece to the others with the screws, the metal melting in his hands, fusing together. The screws were unsightly, so he capped them, hiding every trace of its mechanical function. The glass cylinder slid into the hole at the bottom of the copper tube, sealing its light inside with the small wooden knob.

The buzz subsided in his skull and time moved through him at a regular pace again. He took a deep breath in, unsure of whether he had been breathing at all in the last couple of minutes.

A metallic flower, its petals closed, was the result of his efforts.

Nicholas ran his fingers down the ornament. He pressed a small silver button on its stem, and it jostled the glowing cylinder hidden within. At once, the metallic petals clicked open, yellow sparks bursting from within. The light bounced off the inside of the petals, reflecting it up and outward, lighting the surrounding area.

He was so enamoured by the creation he forgot it was for Sam and only now turned to present it to her. Pulling his eyes from it, he wished he hadn't. Sam had lost all colour in her face. Her eyes were stretched wide, not in amazement, but in terror.

"Sam? What's wrong?" He leaned over the table.

Her body flush with the wall behind her, she gripped a nearby shelf, her knuckles white with tension. She opened her mouth, but nothing came out for several seconds.

Finally, she stammered, "Who was that?"

"What?"

She raised a shaky finger and pointed. She managed a few more words. "Who was it, Nico? Behind you?"

Nicholas, too confused to share her fright, turned around. No one was there. "What are you talking about?" He let his shoulders fall. "You're trying to scare me, aren't you?"

"Nicholas! There was someone standing behind you the whole time!"

Nicholas felt like a fool now, his arm still outstretched, holding the flower.

"Sam, there isn't anyone there."

He set the gift down, the light from it retreating into his hand. The veins in his wrist shone gold for a moment. That was new.

"Nico, there was a man. His arms passed through you. When he moved, you moved, like a puppet."

"A puppet?" Nicholas looked back at all the miscellaneous items he created. "So, you're saying I didn't make any of this myself?" he asked.

She doesn't believe in you.

His head felt hot.

"Nico, your eyes. They're not right. They're glowing. We need to leave," she said.

She stepped back towards the door.

"Sam, wait! I don't know what you think you saw, but there's no one else here. I've told you before I have a way with machines. I can see inside them, how they work. That's how I'm making all this!"

"There was someone there, Nico. We need to leave. This place isn't right."

No!

"No!" Nicholas slammed his fist on the table. A tremor pulsed through the workshop causing the shelves to shake.

Sam jumped. He'd never seen her afraid. Ever. She was now.

"I made these things, Sam! I made them. It's all I have now."

"Nico..."

She's belittling you, the way she always does.

"What do you know? You're probably still drunk." The words flew from his mouth without thought. Nicholas ripped open random shelves and dumped their contents to the floor. "Look! Look! I'm doing this. I'm choosing the materials and the materials are choosing me. You don't believe I'm in control? Watch."

Nicholas returned to the table and his hands went to work. He moved faster than before, fuelled by a rush of anger. In only a moment, he held a silver necklace attached to a blue pendant.

"Still don't believe me, Sam?"

She stared in disbelief. "That's the necklace I lost last year. You made another like it."

"Not like it, Sam. I thought about your necklace and now it's here. This is the actual necklace. Not new, yours!" he roared.

She didn't respond. She cried.

She's worthless.

His eye twitched. The necklace felt heavy in his hand. He wanted to throw it at her. His grip tightened on it.

No. Think of your mother.
Tell her about your mother.

The voice pierced through the sheet of anger. His grip loosened, and the necklace fell to the tabletop. He came out from behind the workbench and stopped a few feet from her. She stepped back from him.

"Sam..."

"Nico?"

"My mother, she's dead."

He broke the way his father did a week earlier. He sobbed and filled his small hands with the rolls of her dress. They both cried, and she squeezed him so tight he couldn't breathe.

"Why do I lose everyone? My sister, my mother."

Sam struggled to hold him up, so she brought him down to the ground and lay his head in her lap.

"Don't take this from me, Sam. This place is all I have now. This is mine and it's all I have now."

Good.
Pathetic.

"You have me. You have your father."

He sat up and slid his arm underneath her hair and around her neck. She winced. He pushed her hair from her shoulder and saw deep blue bruises circling the back of her neck.

He stopped crying. "What happened?"

She swatted his hand away, pulling her hair back down.

"It's nothing. I didn't do well at work and—"

"That man did this, didn't he?"

"I'm fine. I need to follow directions better. There's a lot to learn. It's okay, we're talking about your mother now—"

"Did he hurt you anywhere else?"

Now it was her turn. She pressed her head against the wall and her arms fell limp at her sides. What seemed like months of pent-up emotion spilled from her.

"He makes the other girls do things with men. He hasn't made me yet, but he will soon. He said he'd hurt my family if I leave."

Nicholas took her hand in his and squeezed it.

"Do your mum and dad know?"

She shook her head. "I haven't been home in weeks. It started out fine. I was making money serving drinks, performing on stage for them. Then one night he said I couldn't leave anymore. I haven't seen my parents since. I have to get back. He'll know I left. He'll know I snuck out last night." She rose to her feet.

"Wait, what are you doing? You can't go back!" Nicholas said, standing with her.

"I have to. If I run away, he'll hurt them. The other girls, they told me he'll hurt them."

Nicholas wiped his eyes and face with the back of his sleeve. He took his jacket off and offered it to her to wipe her own tears away.

"I'm going to help you. You're going to get out of there. I promise."

She nodded, but he could tell she wasn't listening anymore. She turned to leave but stepped back and took the necklace from the table.

"Is this really it?"

"It is."

"How do you know?"

"Because it was me who threw your old one in the river."

She sniffled. "I know."

She looked back at him. "Nico, this place isn't right. Go home to your father. He'll be worried about you."

Then she left. The echo of metal sliding against metal bounced off the walls of the workshop.

He ran his finger along the flower he made earlier. It warmed against his skin, then grew cold. He entered the main room and sat down at the desk. He pressed the button again, and the petals fell open. The flower sprang back to life, just long enough for a small spark to light the bottom line of the hidden message.

May you find the tools you need to live up to the name.

CHAPTER THIRTY-FIVE

THE FINE EDGE of the hook in Ned's hand glistened in the firelight. He grabbed a length of rope from his horse and tied it to the loop on its end.

"It's as good an idea as any." He cast a look at Emma and James, then to a window above.

He swung the hook, slow at first, then faster as he grew confident in his creation. It whooshed as it passed his ear. He released it as it came around and it disappeared into the red-lit window, followed by a satisfying clang loud enough to hear from below.

He tugged on the rope. It would hold. Without hesitation, which seemed to surprise his companions, he ran to the wall and climbed. It took only ten vertical steps to make the window. He swung an arm over the sill and pulled himself in.

Red and yellow light bathed the room. Smoke pillowed against the ceiling, rolling across the roof like an angry ocean, swallowing beams like tiny ships. Opposite the door, a group of children huddled in the corner, their beds positioned around them like a wall. He counted seven in total. The smallest looked twelve years old, five boys and two girls.

"Come here!" Ned shouted.

Most of them were hiding their faces in pillows. Others seemed mesmerised by the flames slithering up the walls and the encroaching venomous cloud of black.

Ned stepped towards them, testing each board with his weight before moving on. "We need to leave!"

They heard him this time. Whether he was friend or foe, the suffocating heat convinced them all to trust him. One-by-one, Ned lifted each of them to the window ledge to climb down. Emma met them below once they touched the ground, directing each of them away from the building.

The beds were now engulfed in flame and the room's structure so weak parts of the floor had fallen away. Air shimmered like a reflection in a poorly crafted mirror and the wood around his feet whistled and popped, forcing him back to the window. He leaned his head out.

"Ask them if there are any others!" he screamed.

Emma nodded and turned to the children. They weren't responding. Not even a headshake.

"Ask harder!" The fire licked the fine hairs on the back of his neck.

Emma shook one of the older children and he raised a single finger.

"Shit," he muttered. "Where?" he yelled.

The boy shook his head without an answer.

Ned faced the blaze; it ate away at the walls, exposing adjacent rooms. He screamed into the inferno, calling for an answer, anything to lead him to the remaining child. There was a hollow suck of air as the fire churned under him, waiting for him. He shouted again. The room hissed, and he crouched to stay below the smoke. He pushed a burning table from his path; it slid across the floor into a dresser. The flames swallowed them both. He called out again. His eyes boiled in their sockets like two white potatoes in a bubbling stew.

Ned swore he received an answer. It was only once and could have been a cry as much as the whistle of burning moisture or the clang of a metal tool falling from balance. Did he conjure it himself to push him forward? Overwhelmed, his eyes, nose, and throat stung with the sharp bite of the smoke. There was nothing certain in the yellow and the red except for the yellow and the red. Ned leaped back to the window. Grabbing the rope, he climbed back down. He ran the kids across the river to join the rest of the Luddites.

The fire ate through the factory's wooden veins, leaving the metal, brick and mortar shell intact, its guts exposed, a carcass devoured.

Ned stumbled back to the factory alone.

Every mistaken sizzle and pop from the inferno cut into him deeper and deeper. The expression on the boy's face as he exited without the last child ripped Ned open. Was it a brother or a sister or a friend he'd left behind? He stared into the flames, their avarice unquenchable.

His vision went blurry. He closed his eyes to retreat from it, but his precious gift, the same one that struck him blind, now refused him that same reprieve. The white light etched itself into the back of his eyelids, but his second sight didn't see the flames, but everything touched by them. He looked to the second floor of the factory, and only then did he spot what his mind decided was a glowing mass the size of a child only one room over from the one he'd been in.

His heart wanted him to look away, but he had to be sure. Blood pounded against his skull as he tried to focus on the ball of light. He felt so close to it, close enough to feel the threads of the child's clothes and strands of hair. He reached his hand out to touch, to save, to do anything, but it grasped nothing but molten air. The mass grew smaller and smaller and smaller until the light was no more. And as he tried not to lose sight of it, the fire burned beyond his eyes and enveloped the world in its red hands until all that remained was black and black and black.

CHAPTER THIRTY-SIX

Nicholas played out a dozen conversations with his father in his head, but none of them seemed to provide a satisfying excuse for leaving him alone to bury his mother. The workshop swallowed him, and it wasn't until now that he realized how strange it was for him to have abandoned his father when he did. Even knowing that, it wasn't his top concern. He needed to help Sam, so he needed his father's help.

He took a few items from the workshop. A few baubles he thought might help convince his father of where he'd been. The mechanical flower, which made him uncomfortable now, he left behind. He kept seeing Sam's face stretched in terror whenever he touched it.

Nicholas heaved open the heavy door, which took him to the street, and climbed out. He let the door close and lock under him. A few people eyed him, their stares encouraging him to pull the collar of his coat up around his face.

The wind carried a chill from the night before. Edinburgh looked different to him. Vibrant and fresh with rain, but something else too. He slept here. It was a home away from home and the statues were now less menacing, the alleys brighter, the smells richer.

He set off, phantom pain entering his body once again.

THE EARTH SQUISHED UNDERFOOT, and, in places, small puddles formed. It made the walk slow, which gave him more time to grow anxious. His chest tightened with each step, his body sweating at the uncertainty he'd created for himself. He reached the fork in the road and headed down the path to his hamlet, catching sight of the hill where his people buried everyone who passed. The top would be comforting if not for the cemetery. A massive oak tree with a sturdy trunk grew beside a few dozen graves. Its large, green leaves bathed the hamlet's loved ones in shadow throughout the day. A shovel leaned against it. It could have dug the hole where his mother rested now.

There were dozens of crosses of distinct quality and size. Some were chiselled from stone; others were only sticks tied together with twine. Agata's work. She always contributed decorative touches to the grave markers. It gave each marker uniqueness despite the uniformity of death.

A strong wind snapped a weak branch above him and the memory of Agata snapping his mother's arms intruded on him. He pushed it from his mind.

Nicholas visited his grandmother's grave every year with his mother. The last time was not long ago.

"Death can be messy, Nicholas, but we all look the same in the end, don't we? It can be beautiful when you think of it like that. In time," his mother had said.

It did not feel beautiful to him then, and especially not now.

He knew his family could lay claim to three markers: his grandfather, his grandmother, and his sister. He kept his eyes down, staring at the grass instead, not wanting to see her grave before he needed to.

Finally, he raised his head and now counted four markers for his family.

He took his hat off and clenched it between icy fingers. The wind picked up again.

JOHN LOCHERBIE
1732-1789

"All around on pine tree tops
a little golden light was propped.
And overhead at heaven's gates
my wide eyes saw the Christ child wait."

He did not remember his grandfather, but he heard stories. A serious man, like Nicholas's own father, but more absent. He married his occupation first, his wife second. He remembered his grandmother sitting with her husband for weeks before he died. Laughter spilled from their room often, but the fever still took him.

EUPHEMIA LOCHERBIE
1735-1795

"Friend, sursum corda, soon or slow we part,
like guests who've joyed their fill;
Forget them not, nor mourn them so,
the ghosts we all can raise at will."

After losing her husband, his grandmother was never the same. She laughed and smiled, but her eyes, the same eyes as Nicholas, were deep and sad. The creases around them rarely stretched. He wasn't sure if anyone else sensed her longing to rejoin her husband, but he liked to think she knew he could tell. They shared an unspoken secret that he never wanted to understand.

ELSPETH LOCHERBIE
1786-1794

"They can no longer die; for they are like angels."

His sister's passing was the first death he could comprehend. He understood he wouldn't see her again. His last memory of her was a moment of sibling civility. They had stacked several crates and climbed them to the roof of their home. Nicholas lay down, staring up at the sky, letting his eyes wander the stars. His sister, more apprehensive, ran back inside. He yelled after her, assuming she went to tell his parents and get him into trouble. He wanted to enjoy himself before he was told to come down.

But his parents didn't come. Instead, his sister returned with an armful of biscuits and a tiny jar of jam.

"Nic! I brought food. We can live up here now!" Her eyes sparkled.

It was the first time Nicholas realized his little sister had become his friend. They dipped bread into raspberry jam and Elspeth asked her older brother life's most important questions. She passed only a few months later.

He told no one about that night. He saved it for himself.

Nicholas took a deep breath and knelt in front of the last marker.

CATHERINE LOCHERBIE
1757-1796

"He hath made everything beautiful in its time."

His mother rested only a short distance below. He dug his fingers into the soil. His eyes closed as they grew heavy with tears. He swallowed hard and took a broken breath in. Agata had splashed her cross with paint, bright and cheery. A shell necklace was tied around the marker, a gift he made for his mother after his sister passed, was a pleasant sight. He found the shells in a small box under Elspeth's bed and put a string through them. And here it was again, wrapped around the marker as it had around her neck.

"I'm sorry, Mum. I'm sorry I wasn't here." A wave of guilt hit him in the deepest part of his stomach.

Fix her.

He remembered the words he heard before. They made no sense at the time, but now, with what he'd discovered, could he? Could the workshop make his mother whole again, like Sam's necklace? It was a morbid thought, pointless too. She was beyond his reach now.

He stayed there for several minutes. The only sounds were the wind through his collar and a few passive bleats from nearby sheep. He tugged at the grass, squished the blades between his fingers, staining his skin. He sobbed for a short time, then stood and sniffed away the sadness before retreating to the path.

It was time to go home.

CHAPTER THIRTY-SEVEN

NED DIDN'T SPEAK for two days after the fire. He wandered the wooded areas around the camps they made on their way back to the port of Inverness. The murmurs from the Luddites still reached him. They didn't know where they were going or their purpose. There weren't enough provisions for the trip home, so they restocked in small villages, sending in only a few of their number to not raise suspicion.

They took the orphans with them. A small kindness for burning down their home, but it slowed them down. They camped in small patches of woodland or out in open fields. They made only a few fires, waiting until their clothes and boots soaked through from rain and puddles and dew.

The group grew quiet and sombre. The air around them was thick with guilt, compounded many times over by the man who walked alongside his horse at the front. Ned had to say something, but he couldn't think. The crackle of the fire still pricked his ear, licking his neck even as he put days between it and him. His appetite had left, and he grew weaker and more irritable each day.

He snapped at Emma, even when he tried not to. It didn't deter her, though.

On the third day, she approached him again, surprising him with a light touch on his arm. He jolted.

"Ned," she said. "Ned, what are we doing?"

He didn't know what to say. Even if he did, he didn't want to talk. Instead, the squish of dozens of boots marching through wet earth filled the silence between them.

"Ned, answer me," she said.

Ned stopped and the entire column did the same.

"We're going back to Mousa. Where else can we go?" he said, not turning to her.

She walked around to face him. "Ned, your face. It's bleeding and covered in soot still." She rubbed his cheek with the back of her gloved hand. He winced. She whispered to him now, in a tone he rarely heard. "These people need a leader, Ned. I understand where your mind is, but you need to tell us what we're doing, where we're going, how we're going to get there."

"What did you mean when you said this dagger was always mine?"

"I don't know what I was saying. I was confused when I saw Stuart and Sarah. I still am."

"Don't change the subject, Emma. What did you mean?"

Emma clutched her arm to her side. "I'm sorry, Ned. I wanted to tell you. I did. I just, I was afraid you would remember me."

"Remember you?"

"We've met before. When we were children."

"What are you saying?"

"You were so brave. Not helpful, but you were brave. And in return, I did a horrible thing to you. I thought I'd killed you. Most of my life, I thought I'd killed a young boy for being in the wrong place at the wrong time."

"I don't remember you."

"I know. And that's why this worked. You still have such a

boyish face. When I saw you outside Dundee, I knew it was you. At first, I couldn't believe it, but that thing," she said, nodding towards the dagger, "it lit up like a candle when I pointed it in your direction."

"What does the dagger have to do with me?"

"It's not a dagger. It was a metal flower. I hollowed out the hilt and secured it inside. Suited me better."

Ned opened the end of the dagger and pulled out the light source. It was a flower. He pressed a button on its stem and the petals spread out, a light amber glow emanating from the centre.

"I promised myself I would never put you in harm's way again. I had a second chance, and I took it, Ned. It was selfish and I'm sorry I hid this from you."

"Why didn't you tell me? Emma, you watched me fight for every scrap of memory. You could have given me this. Told me any of this. You had the only thing I wanted, and you kept it from me."

Her eyes reddened, fighting back tears. "If you remembered where we met, what I did, what I did to you, you would never—"

"And that's my choice to make. Not yours. You made the choice for me. You lied to my face every day. You shared my bed, held me when the dread of not knowing overwhelmed me. You could have stopped it." Ned felt his chest tighten. "How can I trust you?"

Emma stared at the ground, not able to meet his eyes. "What made you think you ever could? I robbed you when we met. For the second time. You trusted me then."

"Aye, I suppose that makes me a fool."

Stuart approached, spurred on by the others. Emma turned away.

"Sir, they asked me to find out where we're—"

"We're going back to Mousa. Where else would we go?"

"It's just that things have changed. These people weren't made for what happened at that factory."

"Then leave. Once we reach the coast, they can return to their lives. Give up on this idea. The Luddites will be no more," he spat. "We'll all go our separate ways. We'll all be better off."

Emma cleared her throat. "These people depend on you. You cannot abandon them. They've built their lives around you and this idea. You turned them from craftsmen into soldiers and they raided the factories you pointed them at."

"Factories I pointed them at? You act like they're tools I've used to further my aim. These people came to me! They were angry, and I gave them a direction so they didn't eat each other alive. I'll abandon them in a heartbeat if it saves one boy or girl from suffering the fate of the one we lost in that factory. I'm done with it. We've brought nothing but destruction to a few tiny villages and we have the gall to think we're the ones doing right? It's a lie."

"We're feeling the loss of that boy the same as you. Just because we weren't in the fire doesn't mean we don't grieve the same. You did more than any of us." Emma pointed toward the orphans. "If it wasn't for you, those children would have perished in the fire. You're focused on the one you lost. Ned, you didn't lose a child. You saved seven."

"Emma, I didn't lose one child. I slaughtered four men without even knowing I'd done it. Murdered them. I stoked the anger of these people to coerce them into destroying the lives of others to make up for losing their own. Why? I don't care about any of this. I just had nothing better to do because I didn't know who I was, so I let everyone else decide for me. But you're right, I didn't lose one child—they did!" he said, pointing to the camp.

Emma huffed before leaving him and rejoining the group. Stuart did the same.

He stomped through the mud after them.

"Everybody hear me! I know you're all wondering what we're doing. We're heading toward the coast. Once we're there, you can board the ship and return to the island, but I will not be joining you."

The group murmured.

"I haven't been honest with you. You chose me to lead you based on the assumption that I hated the industries that took your livelihood from you, because I had some vague notion that my mother also lost her job to them. I don't know if that's even true. He might," he pointed to James. "But I think he might be full of shite too. The fact is, I said it to get the job. I wanted purpose. I wanted direction. Something to give my life meaning, but it was a lie, as far as I know."

"Ned, that's enough," Emma said.

"I don't hate these industries. I have no quarrel with the factories or their owners or the machines. The opposite! They fascinate me. The other night, you lot attacked a factory that turned out to be home to several orphans. One of them died in a fire that they set themselves because they feared for their lives. They were so afraid of you that they started a fire to protect themselves.

"I remember little of my childhood, but I can't help but feel lucky if it means I don't have to relive nights like this. They will remember the living, breathing nightmare of a pack of crazed men and women bringing hammers down on everything around them because they're too stubborn, or too stupid, to realise the world is changing."

Emma approached Ned and tried to pull him back from the crowd by the arm.

"Get off me!" Ned shouted and pulled his arm free. "I cannot justify this any longer." Ned walked to his horse, but paused. "When the boat arrives, you will have two options. You can return to the island and rejoin your families and remain there as long as you are able. Mousa is yours. You'll be safe and hidden for as long as you wish. Stay there and grow old with your anger. There'll be no place for you on the mainland."

He glanced at Emma, who was kicking mud from her boots.

"The second choice, because I own my part in all of this, is to continue with me, away from this. I promise no satisfaction. I promise no vengeance. We'll find something new, begin somewhere else. We'll use our skills to bring something better into this world." He stopped to look at James. The man looked older today than any other. "I have a gift, and I refuse to accept that it's meant for destruction and death. That is what I offer. We'll reach Inverness soon. You can make your decision then."

Many of them began whispering to each other, their decisions already made.

Ned returned to his horse, Emma's gaze tracking him like prey.

CHAPTER THIRTY-EIGHT

"FATHER!" Nicholas pushed the front door open a few inches and looked into his darkened home. The light from the doorway allowed him to see inside a short distance, but the shuttered windows ensured anything beyond that remained in shadow. A damp musk wafted towards him.

"Father? Are you here?"

He took a few slow steps into the house. His eyes adjusted to the low light and the large table at the far end of the room where his family ate dinner—used to eat dinner—came into view. Dishes set out for a meal that never happened sat neatly on its top.

His father didn't work Sundays, but if he wasn't here, he could be doing any number of things. The stove was cool, empty of fresh ash or embers. No one had used it in at least a day. The sheets on his bed were still in disarray. They probably hadn't been touched since he left.

He tiptoed around his own home before taking a deep breath to relax. His stomach dropped as his hope turned to worry.

Nicholas took a seat beside the stove, wondering what to do

next, and resolved to stay put. When his father returned, he would be here.

The house didn't feel like a home to him now. The furniture, its trappings, all tied to memories of things he already buried deep within him. He no longer wanted a connection to this place. The workshop pulled him towards something new, something better. Nothing here changed, or ever would. He kicked the stove, watched the ash tremble. He noticed a small area on its top, rectangular, clean of dust, like something was placed here, then taken. Whatever it was, wasn't there any longer. So many things felt missing or wrong to him now.

He stared into the cold fire pit and the guilt and bewilderment of his leaving when his father needed him most flooded over him.

Nicholas decided he would tell him about the Dollmaker, the workshop, the man on the horse, and all the things he created. They would get Sam back together. He breathed easier already.

He'd wait for his father.

CHAPTER THIRTY-NINE

When they arrived at the northeastern town of Inverness, the group dragged themselves to the harbour. It was midday, and the townsfolk milled about through narrow, worn streets, always under the sun-stirred shadow of Inverness Castle. Hoping to avoid drawing attention, the Luddites stuck to the perimeter, making their way around to the Firth harbour. Some trailed behind. Ned wondered if he'd lose a few of them on their way, parting before they had to say goodbye. The majority made their way to the water and fell to the wet sand, relieved to be still for the first time in weeks.

"They're undecided, all of them," Emma said, walking up beside Ned.

"Not all of them," he replied. "There's less here than when we started."

"You can't blame them, Ned."

"I don't blame them. I gave them options. Both of which are better than fending for themselves."

"And which is the better of your options?"

Ned kicked at a seashell with the toe of his boot, dislodging it from the sand. Moisture filled the crevice it left. "Are you asking for them or are you asking for yourself?"

"You brought me in to guard you, Ned," she responded. "I go where you go."

"Duty. Is that what we've come to?"

"I don't know what we've come to," she hissed.

Ned pulled the dagger from his belt and, pulling her hand towards him, placed it in her palm. "I've been thinking—"

"Ned, I wanted to tell you every day."

He put his hand up. "Let me finish. It sounds to me like you made a poor decision as a child and you made a second one to erase the first." He sighed. "More importantly, that also means you're the only one who's known me my whole life and you're still here, willing to die for me, no less." He closed her fingers around the hilt of the dagger. "I only care for who you are, not who you were."

She put the dagger back on her belt and held Ned tight, the waves muffling their emotions.

He pulled Emma down to the sand with him. She fell in a reluctant heap. "So, I'll ask again, love, are you asking for them or are you asking for yourself?"

She stayed quiet for several moments, trying to pull his plans from him without having to ask the question. "Both."

Her hair whipped across her face as the wind flew towards the sea, carrying its thick saltiness in the air for a moment.

"The island will become a tomb for those who stay, as it has for others," Ned said.

"How do you know this?"

"I know it. You know it too. They all do. Other bounty hunters will find us. The reward for a small army of Luddites will guarantee they are never safe. Someone will have spotted us, figured out who we are."

"Then what's your alternative?" She crossed her arms.

Ned tucked the seashell back into its spot in the sand; only the faintest trace of it having moved remained. He kicked sand on top of it, covering it from view.

"I've thought about it, and I want to give them meaningful work. Something good can come from that fire. There are orphans like the ones we found in the factory all over Scotland. We could help them."

"You want to adopt all the orphans of Scotland?"

"Would that scare you?" he asked, a grin breaking on his face.

She pushed him away.

"No, of course we can't adopt them all, but we can make their lives bearable, show them they aren't alone."

"How would we do that?"

Ned pointed to the Luddites. "Them. All of them. Seamstresses, cobblers, weavers, carpenters, whole industries right here in front of us. We could make clothes, shoes, toys! We could make them toys, Emma. Look at the children we brought with us. They've got nothing but pyjamas and worn-out boots, and we gave them the boots. Not a single one of them took an important keepsake with them, something from a lost parent, something they found, something given to them. Children should never have nothing. We can't adopt them all, but we can sure as hell clothe them and give them a reason to smile."

Emma's arms fell at her side, her shoulders relaxing.

Ned laughed. "I didn't want to tell you because I feared you'd think me mad."

She wrapped her arms around his neck. "So, a man and woman with no children of their own will provide for all the lost children of Scotland?"

"For now. Maybe we can do better than that."

"Better than that?" Emma kissed him. The tide rose and threatened to dampen their feet, but she held it.

"How will we pay for this?"

Ned, full of purpose, rose and pulled his sword from the

scabbard hanging from his horse. "We're not going to pay for any of it. He is," he said, staring at his father.

Ned marched toward James. The old man was on his knees in the sand, his hands tied behind his back. Despite his vulnerability, James stared him down as he approached. The sea air tousled his loose hair about his face. A short beard hid his chin now.

"Have you decided to let her kill me, then?"

Ned shook his head.

"I have questions and a proposition. If you answer my questions truthfully, then we'll discuss the proposition."

"And if you feel my answers do not contain enough truth?"

"Let's assume that isn't an option."

James nodded. "Let's begin."

"What are we?"

"I don't know of a name, if there ever was one. My father was like this, and so was his. It affects the first-born of each generation. We can achieve strange things. Things that shouldn't be possible."

"So, you can do everything I can?"

"We don't all share the same gifts, but we can each access the workshop. The place you went when you came back with the hook. We can all go there. We can create anything we can think of and so many more things we would never even dream."

"Why?"

"I don't know. My father explained to me that we choose our own path. Some use it for good, others not. You might even recognise the names of some of our ancestors if I told you, but I wouldn't want to influence you."

"And you? What do you do with your gifts?"

"Nothing of note. Made a small fortune with minor crimes. Tried to walk a line between being human and being more than human. I don't want to make a name for myself. I don't think many people would care to know someone like me exists."

"Why'd you find me?"

"I knew that if you were still alive, you would need someone to help you along, as my father did. So, I never gave up trying to find you. I always kept an ear out."

"See, that bothers me. What could you have heard that would tip you off? No one knows my identity, least of all myself. At most, you might learn of the location of the Luddite General, assuming you were looking for him. What would make you assume I am your son?"

"We'll call it a hunch."

"We'll call it more than that or I turn you over to Emma."

James looked downward at the sand. Bits of rock crystal whipped around him. "This may not satisfy you, but it's one of my gifts. I sense the hearts of men, their true intentions. Their pasts, their possible futures. It's not exact, but it's rarely wrong. When I met the merchant in Edinburgh, I felt you in him. He was connected to you. That connection created a tether that pulled me to Mousa."

"So, the plan was to find me, help me learn to use these gifts, and then what? We rob markets for coin like bandits?"

"No, you do whatever you want. I wanted to make sure my son knew who he was."

Ned took a spot on a large rock facing the water. "How many gifts will I receive?"

"You might gain many more, or no more at all."

"The workshop, how do I go there?"

"It gets easier over time, but you think it and you will be there. I've become so adept that I can reach into it with a hand and pull out what I need, never even leaving the spot."

"Could you do that now? Reach in for a knife and cut the rope around your wrists?"

James risked a smile. "I could. That wouldn't be very honest of me, though."

"So, right now I can see through physical space, including several moments into the past and future. I will be able to transport to any location at will, and I can access a workshop that can create anything I need."

"It would seem so."

"What do I do with that, James?"

"Whatever you wish."

"I'll tell you what I'm thinking, but you're going to laugh."

"Try me."

He pointed his chin towards the orphans playing on the beach. "I want to help them. I want to bring them toys and clothing and shoes."

"Ned, we can do that right now without your gifts."

"No, all of them. Every boy and girl just like them. I can use the workshop to create designs. The Luddites can make them. I'll use my gifts to deliver them all over Scotland, maybe farther."

James frowned. "The toys?"

"The toys. And clothes."

"That's certainly one option."

Ned crouched in front of James.

"The problem is that I would need funding to pay my workers a fair wage. We would need food, shelter. That doesn't come cheap."

"No, it doesn't, but with your gifts you could—"

"Take it from others? Precisely what I'm thinking. In fact, I think I might pay for everything by taking it from a single person."

An expression of knowing crossed James's face. "Ah, I should have seen that coming."

"It strikes me that a man with a lifelong quest to find his son must have gained significant wealth to do so. And since it seems likely you took the coin in less than legal ways, I don't think you'd mind if I redistribute it to people who are more deserving?"

"Happy to help..." James said.

"Good. I'll ignore your lack of enthusiasm." Ned stood. "James, I'll be honest with you. I still don't trust you, but something has brought us together. I'm willing to find out why."

Ned slit the ties around James's hands with the tip of his sword.

James grunted his approval and massaged the inflamed skin around his wrists.

"I'll take what I can get then," he said. James pulled an old, yellow-stained envelope from his pocket, thinned by wear. "I wasn't sure if I should give this to you. I thought it might confuse things, but if it helps lessen your doubts, I want you to have it. Read it the next time you're alone. It might not tell you anything new, but I wrote it the day I lost you. That should count for something."

James grabbed Ned's arm and placed it in his palm. He patted him on the shoulder and his father left him standing on the beach alone.

CHAPTER FORTY

NICHOLAS WAITED FOR TWO DAYS, but his father never returned. He couldn't have gone far, but no one in the hamlet recalled seeing him leave. Several people worried, including Agata.

He returned to his home and sat in silence at the kitchen table. The breeze picked up, and the shutters slapped back and forth, squeaking on rusted hinges. He thought about lighting the stove but couldn't muster the desire. Instead, he leaned back in his chair and let it creak against the thrashing of the wind. A painting of his father's hung opposite him. Nicholas never saw him paint, but he claimed to do so in his youth. This one was a large stone structure on an island he visited, the Broch of Mousa he called it. It lay further north than Nicholas had ever been and ever wanted to be.

His eyes swept across the swirls of paint, searching for the beginning and the end of waves, marvelling at the easy transition of blue to green, water to land. He fell down a crevasse in the canvas, created by large, chunky, grey paint splotches his father used to recreate the stones of the Broch. The wind outside grew more rapid and sharp, chilling him. He must have left a window open. His eyes were stuck to the painting, and he found it difficult to look away. He spotted a rusted iron gate cut into the side of the stone monolith. It clanked in the wind and the ocean spray refreshed his skin.

It wasn't until he heard distant thunder that Nicholas realised he was no longer looking at a painting of the Broch of Mousa, but that he was standing in front of it. The structure towered over him, dominating the darkening sky. The ocean roared behind him and he stumbled back, tripping over loose rocks. A sharp pain shot up his legs and he took a hard fall but righted himself. His mind reeled. He panicked. Lightning arced its way from the clouds to a spot out on the water. The sudden flash frightened him, and he ducked for cover under the rocky overhang protruding above the rusted gate he marvelled at earlier. He gripped the bars in his small hands. They were cool and wet, and bits of orange flaked away at his touch. It wasn't locked though. He pushed against it and the door creaked and swung open.

He scurried inside, away from the coming storm. Inside, the Broch offered little cover. Its top open to the sky, rain spotted the earthen floor. A covered staircase around the perimeter wall led to the top.

Nicholas sat on the stairs and leaned against the wall. His small body shook with fear and cold. The events of the last week finally overwhelmed his mind and he felt himself slipping away, loosening, as if he became unstuck in the world. It was an uncomfortable sensation, but one he welcomed if only because it allowed him to ignore everything around him. He shivered and pulled his coat tight. It had been days since he lost Sam and he worried that he'd fail her. He came home for help and now found himself on an island, alone. The rain pitter-pattered against the exterior of the stone structure before it rose into an awful din. The storm tore across the small island and Nicholas huddled into a damp corner, burying his head into his knees, unable to understand what was happening to him.

CHAPTER FORTY-ONE

THERE WERE VERY few defining moments in Ned's life that he remembered. Taking charge of the Luddites and meeting Emma were the only ones to come to mind. Holding this letter in his hands, he couldn't help but feel he was about to add another to a very short list.

The rest of the pub's patrons were off in a corner, and he found a lone seat by the hearth.

He braced himself and opened the envelope. The slip of paper inside was discoloured. It was written in his father's hand. It looked so much like his own.

Son,

I buried your mother this morning. Agata did not want to leave it any longer. I could have tried harder to make her wait, but I'm not sure I wanted that either.

If you read this, know that I'm not angry you left. I do understand. I wonder why I don't do the same. Moving on from this place might be best for both of us. First, there are things I need to show you that I should have done long ago.

Your grandfather told me once that the best life is one where you don't try too hard and don't try too little. You do just enough to avoid looking back at the end. I'm not sure if that's the best advice, but know that I often catch myself looking back.

I hope to see you soon, but if for some reason we do not find one another again, try harder than I did and know that I love you no matter who you become.

May you find the tools you need to live up to your name.

Your father

Edinburgh, 1796

Ned traced the final inked letters with his fingertips. The paper crinkled under the pressure, and he slid it back into the envelope, holding it steady as if the ink would run from the page if tipped.

His hands shook, still blue with ocean chill, but he felt a warmth he had never known.

CHAPTER FORTY-TWO

"I WILL NEVER, ever marry you, Nicholas Locherbie."

Sam's face burned into his memory that night. Last summer, their parents let them stay outside in a tent, which was nothing more than a few blankets and a bearskin stretched across some crates.

Nicholas was always fond of Sam. That she was the only girl he knew around his age helped things along. Nicholas tried for her heart every Saturday. And every Saturday, Sam crushed him.

It was the first night they were allowed to stay up as late as they wanted, as long as they didn't complain about their chores the next day. They could smell the coming rain, but it hadn't stopped them. His father helped build a small fire before Sam arrived and Nicholas was in the middle of taking credit for it when she blurted out this Saturday's feelings on matrimony. She was particularly direct this evening. She usually let Nicholas hit a crescendo before bringing him back down.

It worked out for the better. They sat by the dwindling flames and talked instead. Not about anything important, but only of everything that mattered.

"I jumped into the river from the highest branch on the old oak tree today," Nicholas said while he poked the fire with a knotted twig.

"It's about time. I've been doing that for two summers already," Sam said.

"You're two years older than me, so it's the same."

"I guess."

A cool breeze lifted the corners of one of the tent's blankets and a chill ran up Nicholas's pant leg. He moved closer to Sam, who sat with her knees pulled up to her chin, arms locked around them, and leaned against her, back-to-back.

"Do you think it's going to rain?" she asked.

"Probably."

"Will you stay here if it does?"

Nicholas thought about it and saw nothing wrong with the idea. He was sure the bearskin and tree branches could hold out against any storm.

"I will."

"Do you promise?" She turned her head over her shoulder.

"Aye, I do."

"Good. Because I'm not leaving until I've been awake for a full day. You ever stay awake for a full day?"

"Lots of times."

"No, you haven't," she said.

"You don't know everything about me."

She sighed. "Yes, I do."

Sam found a small stick and dragged a line through the dirt.

The fire burned down to some steady coals that fed off one another; the occasional stray breeze brought them to bright life every so often.

"How's your mother, Nico?" Sam asked.

"Good."

"She didn't look good."

"It's her bones. They get stiff when it's going to rain, that's all."

"Is it?"

He didn't answer.

"That sounds terrible," she said.

"She has fine days, and she has bad days. Sometimes the bad days are terrible," he said.

A corner of the tent lifted again by a strong wind, and it blew some debris inside the covering, including a cornflower removed from its stem. The wind almost pushed it into the coals when Sam snatched it up. She spun the flower at its base between her finger and thumb, spreading apart the cornflower's white petals.

She pulled her hair back and slid the flower in above her ear. "Sometimes the bad days are terrible," she repeated.

–

Sam's words echoed around Nicholas, louder than the storm. He cried, his desperation taking over. It was then, surrounded by a sea storm on an island he only ever saw in a painting, that he felt himself pulled home. Pulled, then pushed. His mind went first. He only hoped his body would follow.

CHAPTER FORTY-THREE

NED SPENT the entire evening at a tavern getting drunk, the small room empty now. A stern barmaid did her rounds, kicking the stragglers out. Spotting Ned in the corner, she sighed and made her way to him.

"Do you need a personal invitation? We're closing. Drink up what's left and get on home to your wife."

"I don't have a wife. I mean, I have a woman, but she ain't my wife." Ned hiccupped.

The barmaid took a seat at Ned's table as she wiped it down with a stained rag. "Whatever she is to you, I'm sure she'd love to have you keeping her warm rather than one of my stools. Come on now, I have a headache and you aren't making it any better," she said.

The barmaid stood and pulled a small package from her apron and unwrapped it. Two papelates fell out. She motioned to Ned, and he reached out to grab one, but she snatched it away as his fingers brushed her palm. "I'll share if you agree to roll yourself out and save me the hassle."

He chuckled. "I almost had it." He pushed himself back from the table and stood up, his knees wobbled.

She struck a match and held it against the papelate until it smoked. She inhaled deep and massaged her temple as she let the smoke escape her lungs. "Well, thinking you have something and actually having it are two very different things."

Ned paused, her words igniting some far-off memory. His mind sharpened, pushing through the ale. "Miss, have we met before?"

She looked him up and down. "No, and don't get sweet with me. I'm old enough to be your ma. Seriously, my head is pounding. Make it easy on—"

"Meredith? Is your name Meredith?"

That got her attention. She nodded, taking another long puff and blowing the smoke back at Ned.

"This will sound strange, but I remember working with you at a cotton mill in New Lanark. I was just a child."

"I worked with a lot of children at that mill. I don't remember you."

"It's okay, it was for a day, less than that. I just remember you slowed the loom down for me."

She arched an eyebrow.

"It was kind of you, is all."

"You're welcome," she said, extinguishing the papelate on the table. "Now if you'll excuse me, I do have a warm body I'd like to get home to."

Ned shook his head, still groggy. "Right, I'll leave."

From behind him, she said, "Here, as promised." She grabbed his arm and held his hand in hers as she pressed the small roll of tobacco into his.

Her hands were so warm, and their heat entered him. Before he could say another word, something snapped deep inside. An echo inside his head buzzed the tiny bones in his inner ear. He grew warm and for a time, Ned couldn't swallow. His jaw locked. His grip on Meredith's hand tightened and her face stretched into a panic.

With a splintering crack that first seized his spine and then coursed through every bone in his body, he became as lightning. An energy flowed from him and to him. The stars in the sky were near to him, touchable. His hands passed through their celestial bodies and pink and green and blue gas wisped around his fingertips. He touched planets, breathed their dust, let the flames of a sun, dozens of suns, lick the bottoms of his feet. He felt everything, all things, reach out and cry to him, touch him. All of humanity that lived and ever lived shouted a single syllable that crushed his insides and built him anew. Then all these things withdrew, and he pulled back to the pub; the sensation lasting for but a moment.

On his knees now, beside the table, panting, burning, the hair on his arms singed and the accompanying nauseating scent filling his heaving lungs, the barmaid was no longer with him.

CHAPTER FORTY-FOUR

Nicholas opened his eyes. The workshop. He was conscious, but not inside his body. A peculiar sensation rippled through his mind, like dough flattened by a roller. His edges stretched. Still, he was aware of his body, back on the island. He inhabited both of his selves, one cold and lonely, the other warming and confused.

He made his way into the workshop, drawn into it. The room looked unfamiliar. Spectral shapes glided through the table, through the walls and the shelves. It surprised him, but he wasn't afraid of them. He sensed a kinship. This was family. He understood this place simply by being here. These people came before him.

The flower he made Sam caught his eye, left behind on the table. It glowed a faint blue.

He was being watched, but not by the other spirits that roamed the room. Beyond the far edge of the table, a figure leaned against the wall. They were cast in complete shadow, but after stepping forward, they took on an amber hue. How do you greet a spirit?

Just when he was about to offer his best attempt, he was struck by the sharp smell of coal. The man's eyes sparkled as they took notice of Nicholas.

"Father?"

The shape, the size, the features all belonged to him. His father stared down at him and even in his brilliant state, Nicholas could see he was crying. Still crying.

Nicholas leaped over the table to reach the visage of his father, but once there his hands passed through him like he was made of dust. The arms split apart, their insides sparkling like stars, before reforming.

"Nicholas, I'm sorry," his father said. His voice had a slight echo to it.

"What happened? How are you here? Why can't I..." he trailed off as he waved his hand through his father's, watching it fall apart again.

"This is my fault."

Nicholas scrunched his face in utter confusion. "What do you mean? I need you to help me find Sam. She's in danger and there's a man—"

"Nicholas, wait. I cannot come with you. I cannot leave this place."

Nicholas dropped his arms to his side, took a step back.

"Listen to me, son." He sighed. "There are so many things I should have told you."

"Are you real? Where are you?"

"I am. I'm..."

"Why can't I touch you?"

"Nicholas, please, I need to—"

"You're dead. Just like them, aren't you?" Nicholas said, looking around at the other spirits gliding through the walls of the workshop. "Just like... Mother."

His father nodded.

"Is she with you?"

"No, she isn't."

"Did you—how did you…"

"I wish I had more time to explain. This place, the workshop, it's your birth right. A legacy from a parent to their child, but only one can control it at a time. Once the child enters the workshop, the parent loses command of it and becomes a part of it. We share our knowledge, every one of us," he said, motioning to the gold and blue figures coming and going around them, "with the next of us. I'm sharing everything I learned with you, so are they."

Nicholas stopped breathing as the words sank in. "So, I…"

"It isn't your fault. I should have explained this to you, and I underestimated your ability to find this place without me. I don't understand how…"

Nicholas tried to hold back tears. "A man on a horse led me here. He gave me the key. He showed me where it was. I didn't mean to do this. I didn't know."

"This is not your fault." His father knelt to look him in the eye. "Tell me you understand this."

Nicholas nodded through tears.

"Say it, Nicholas."

"I understand," he whispered back. "Were you here when I found it?"

"Aye."

"Why didn't you come to me then?"

"I tried. So hard. Sam saw me. I gave her a fright, though."

"That was you! So, she was right? I'm not building these things myself?"

"You are, Nicholas. I helped you get there faster. We all did."

A chill ran up Nicholas's arm and he remembered why he was here. "I was on an island. I am on an island. Your painting at home, I'm inside it," Nicholas said, wiping his tears.

"Ah, the Broch. You're not in the painting. You're there, the painting gave you enough of an idea to get you there and, even though you might have a hard time controlling it now, you can move great distances in an instant. You have everything you need to leave that island. And everything you need to help Sam."

"I have nothing, though. I don't have anyone to help me. I don't even know where she is."

"But you do. You have all those things and more. Tell me what you feel when you think of Sam."

"She's in danger."

"That's not a feeling. Tell me what you feel when you think of your friend."

"I'm scared."

"Ignore the fear. Why are you scared for her?"

"She's my friend. I care about her and I want her to be safe."

"Stay with that. Always ignore the fear. Fear is not the emotion; it is the symptom of something else. If you rid yourself of it, you can focus on what's left. And what's left is usually a good thing."

"That doesn't help me, though."

"I'll show you." His father pointed towards the metal flower. "It glows blue because it is inert. It is an object not yet connected to anyone, but that it glows blue means it can link to someone with a connection to it. Listen to me now, Nicholas."

He nodded to his father.

"There is a gift for everyone, and everyone has a gift. Touch the flower and think of Sam. Do not be afraid for her. Push out the fear and think only of how you feel about her."

Nicholas reached towards the flower and gripped its cool edges between his fingers. He wrapped them tight around the stem and it went from blue to a faint yellow light, warming in his skin.

Once again, a pull came from deep within him.

"I think I'm leaving," he said.

His father smiled.

"Wait! I don't want to leave you!"

"You aren't leaving. You're always here. So am I."

"Can we talk more later?"

"We will. Later."

Nicholas smiled, then the workshop faded from view and was replaced with the raging waters outside the Broch of Mousa. His mind slid back to his body before launching from that desolate space like a rock from a sling.

CHAPTER FORTY-FIVE

NED STUMBLED from the tavern into the street. He crashed hard on one knee, his mind still reeling from his experience.

"Emma!" He did not know where she was, but it was his first instinct. "Emma!"

A voice shouted back from a darkened window, telling him to shut his gob.

What had he done? He wasn't blind and Meredith was nowhere to be seen. This was different. All the fine hair on his body, the visible and invisible, was straight and buzzing. The cuffs of his jacket sleeves were black, as if they'd been lit on fire and put out. The scent of sulphur hung in his nostrils. His eyes stung. In his confusion, Ned stumbled down a nearby pier, tripped, and fell headlong into the water.

He howled as his skin met the icy River Ness. No matter how much he fought, there was no escaping the water. He thrashed in the river, unnoticed by a sleeping Inverness. His boot brushed a rock or a fish or a crate under the water, and for an instant he recalled Emma teaching him to swim.

–

"Kick your feet, Ned! Kick them harder!" Emma called to him from an unseen spot on land.

Ned splashed around in a small inlet. Save for his awkward slapping of the water, it was a quiet and warm afternoon. The commotion drove off the gannets perched on nearby red rocks. He made a show of it for a few seconds longer to convince Emma he tried. Once it was obvious, he moved his body in a fashion that somehow brought him back to dry land.

Crawling towards Emma, the weight of his waterlogged clothes dragging him down, he rolled to his back and said, "I am not fond of that. Not fond of that at all."

Emma laughed.

"Is this necessary?"

"Necessary? Ned, you're in a boat almost every day. It's only a matter of time until one of them sinks. So yes, it is necessary."

Ned wiped the scum from his eyes and from around his mouth.

"It's a silly thing, swimming. It's dangerous enough just to live as we are, but we choose to make it even more difficult by not breathing, just to explore a few dirty lakes."

"Oceans are more than dirty lakes."

"Aye, well, let me know when we see one o' those then."

–

And with that thought, Ned found himself suspended above one. The river was no more, the tavern gone. In fact, there was no land of any kind. He fell downward through the air and smacked into the surface of endless water. His ribs cracked.

It was darker than he thought it would be and he sank faster than he thought he would. He kicked, flailed his arms, tried to grab anything, but he continued to sink, fall. It was all the same. Panic seized him. At the moment between when Ned's face was thrust so violently into the surface of the ocean that the bone around his eyes cracked to now, when he was surrounded by nothing but darkness, he knew eternity.

And in this state, his mind did not reveal his entire life to him. Instead, it pointed only to one of a handful of memories, one in which he made a decision that affected his current chance of survival.

He did not know how to swim.

Eternity was not only timeless, it was cruel. It was also hot, and it was white, and it was terrifying. It was neither quick nor slow, but painful in a way that the body would not understand, and the mind was not prepared for. And he lived it over and over, in multitudes, as if time compacted this moment, folding it over on itself to make it last a little longer. He didn't notice when it finally ended.

CHAPTER FORTY-SIX

NICHOLAS SAW ARTHUR'S Seat rising in the distance as his body traversed space in an instant before settling back in Edinburgh. He caught himself behind a large manor that felt as dominating as the city's castle. Piano keys spilled soft melodies from a large, open window, accompanied by a delicate voice. Nicholas crept to the window. The grade rose towards the home, and it was high enough for him to see through a small crack in the curtains.

The singer was young, Nicholas's age, even. Several men sat in front of her in gold-trimmed chairs covered in red velvet cushions.

Nicholas wrapped the tips of his fingers around the cold ledge and stood on his tiptoes to get a better look into the room. The young girl singing wore a dress like Sam's, only yellow, with a neckline that plunged lower than any dress Nicholas had ever seen. The bodice squeezed her already tiny frame into something inhuman. She continued to sing, her hands pressed against her stomach. Her face was smooth and powdered white save for her blushed cheeks. Her mouth and the tiny muscles in her neck stiffened and relaxed under her skin as she sang.

The song wisped through the cracks in the frame around the

window. It was haunting and comforting at the same time. He couldn't quite make out the lyrics, but it didn't stop him from being soothed by her pitch and the lulls of the song.

The enchantment broke soon after as a commotion came from the chairs in front of her. One man raised a golden paddle. The other men around him applauded with an air of apathy. The young girl half-smiled and bobbed a curtsy towards the man holding the paddle. He stood from his seat and motioned the girl to come to him. She approached, looking back with a nervous glance. Sliding her arm through the one offered to her by the gentleman with the paddle, they left the room.

Nicholas's knees ached and he let himself down. Sam had to be here, but he needed a way in. But how? The building dwarfed most flats in Edinburgh.

The kitchen, Nicholas. Go now.

As the words passed through him an intense pressure formed inside his head. He buckled and fell against the rocky wall, a sharp pain catching him. He froze. The voice spoke his name. He preferred to think of all of this as the result of an overactive imagination, but he couldn't deny it now. Someone was talking to him, leading him. Was it his father? No, he would have told him. After a few moments, it dulled and subsided. In a single breath, his muscles relaxed, and his lungs went to work intaking air and coughing out the trauma.

"What's happening to me?" His words thudded against the wall opposite him.

A door, only a few paces from where he sat, flew open and a serving girl stepped out carrying a large pot. She emptied it on the ground. He laboured over and grasped the knob after she closed it behind her, hoping it wasn't locked. A hard turn popped the door open.

A smear of black and white uniforms busied themselves in the room beyond. Nicholas stood stunned for a moment at the number of serving staff in the kitchen. They were preparing enough food to feed dozens of guests. A long, wooden table stretched out in front of him. It ran through the centre of the kitchen; finished meals gleamed on sparkling plates along its length. The servers, all consumed with their tasks, had their backs turned to Nicholas. A cake, five layers high, took the focus of a man just inside the entry. So ornate, delicate lace and beads draped around the glistening cream.

Nicholas slinked past the workers into a connecting hallway.

An elegant staircase rose out of sight at the far end. The hall was dark, a gold-leaf pattern set into its walls, which bore a strip of cherry wood that ran along their base, breaking only for three doors on either side. The ones on his right were all connected to the kitchen, so he turned to the ones on his left, trying to get away from the traffic.

Each door had a thin panel near the top that could be slid open. They were too high for Nicholas to reach. He'd seen them before, but only ever to see outside. These ones allowed people to see inside the room beyond. Even more curious were the golden nameplates above the doorknobs. The one closest to him read "Edine."

Sam might have her name on one of these too! Pulling the flower out of his coat pocket, he pointed it down the hall. It lit up brighter than ever. He was close.

Move.

The voice disturbed him again. His head lit up, spiked with pain. The hallway rushed past him, he saw nameplates on doors he hadn't reached yet, his vision somehow moving several steps ahead of his body.

I will find her for you.

Ignoring the voice, he shook his head and pushed himself down the hallway. The nameplates matched the ones he had just seen in his mind. Lucy, Fenedril, Adaira. No Samantha.

Reaching the opening of the hallway, he stumbled into the main entry. There was no one else in sight. Not a sound. He couldn't even hear noise from the kitchen or from outside. More cherry wood bannisters framed a wide staircase, its steps fashioned from white marble. Bluish veins ran through the rock giving it an almost smoky texture. Nicholas had never seen such opulence.

He slinked across the space, careful to take most of his steps on the lush, red carpet that flowed down from the second floor. His legs were aching already and as he crossed the runner, his foot caught its edge. He tumbled forward, his fall cushioned and silenced by the carpet, but he felt a crunch beneath him.

The flower had snapped, the stem broken from the assembly. It still worked, but it was awkward to hold.

She's here, she's—oh no. No, no, no.

The voice sounded panicked, unlike the single words and short phrases it used up to this point.

What has he done?

"Stop talking to me," Nicholas said, tired of the rambling in his head.

I'm sorry, Nicholas.
This is not your fault.
It's mine.

"No more!" he screamed before catching himself.

Everything went silent again, including his thoughts.

He'd check the remaining doors on the main floor before heading up to the second floor. He spotted one for Isla and Maidie, still no Samantha. As he ventured down the hall, he heard a conversation coming from one of the doors behind him.

"I have never in all my years heard a song as sweet as yours, my dear," a deep, throaty voice said from beyond the door.

"Thank you, sir," a girl replied.

"Nonsense, call me Papa. How old are you, luv?"

"Nine."

The voices grew louder as they approached the door. Nicholas grabbed the handle of the girl's room closest to him and skittered inside, closing the door behind him.

An abundance of colour struck him. It was so bright he could barely focus on any one thing. The walls were soft pink with thin, white pinstripes running from floor to ceiling. Turning his gaze to the massive bed on the left side of the room, his eyes lifted to a shear lavender sheet draped across the high bed posts like a canopy. The cloth enclosed the bed on either side and billowed at its base. Eight white pillows of all sizes were stacked at the head. The smallest one sat in the middle of the pile; the name "Emma" was stitched into it.

Nicholas scrambled for a spot to hide as the pair approached the door. Piles of plush, stuffed animals, a vanity, and a rocking horse, its straw mane hung still, waited for a child to bring it to life. All of it useless. A large wardrobe opposite the bed was the only option.

A clank from behind startled him and the door opened a crack.

"Thomas!" shouted a second man.

"What is it now?" he asked.

"You remember the rules, do you not?" the second man asked.

"Rules? Of course, I know the rules!" he said.

"Then do follow them this time."

The man huffed and pushed into the room in a hurry, bringing with him a boisterous energy that felt out of place here.

Nicholas found space in the enormous wardrobe to stay out of sight, but he left the panel open a crack. It was enough for him to see the bed and a reflection in the vanity mirror. A girl in a yellow dress entered and he recognised her as the one singing earlier. She lingered at the door. Nicholas could only see the midsection of the man who entered, his reflection cut off.

"Follow me, princess." Spinning around he took the room's contents in. He threw his hands out to either side in an almost welcoming display. "Well, that ol' bastard doesn't disappoint, does he?"

All excitement left the man's body when he noticed the girl's lack of enthusiasm.

"Well now, this won't do, Emma," he said with little energy.

The small girl took a deep breath and life seemed to pour into her makeup-white face like milk filling a glass jug. She spun around, a smile seeming to form a little more with each degree of her turn. She faced the man now; Nicholas could only see her back. She held her hands there. Her left cradled in her right, squeezing it hard.

"That's better, luv."

He took his hat off and gestured towards the bed, "Would you mind if I sat on your bed, Emma? There are no other chairs, I see."

"Of course, Papa," she said with a graceful motion.

The man moved towards the foot of the bed and hung his hat on a hook protruding from one of the bedposts before sitting down, moving into Nicholas's view. The quilt depressed under his weight and the light in the room struck the man at an unflattering angle, his skin blotchy and red.

It was Mr. Chapman. What was he doing here?

Beads of sweat made a few stray curls of his thinning hair so damp they pressed flat like sickly veins on his forehead.

"Come here to me, Emma," he said, wiping his forehead with the back of his shirtsleeve, stained yellow from habit.

Emma moved one foot forward and paused.

"I'd like to play on my rocking horse, Papa," she said as she pulled the same foot back behind her. She tiptoed towards the wooden horse, moving as though she half expected the man on the bed to protest. He didn't.

The rocking horse remained out of Nicholas's view, but he could hear the wood creak as it rocked back and forth, an eerie sound against the heavy quiet of the room. Mr. Chapman sat motionless, his head tilted, rapt watching her teeter on the miniature horse. A smile formed at the corner of his mouth, or it may have just been the way the light stretched a few minor shadows against his face.

They stayed this way for a few minutes. Emma rocked and Mr. Chapman watched from the bed, occasionally wiping the sweat from his brow.

"Emma, that's enough playtime. Why don't you come and sit with me, and I'll tell you a story."

The creaking continued.

"Emma? Come along now. Come here."

Still, the creaking persisted.

"Would you like me to sing for you, Papa?"

Mr. Chapman's lips went tight, and his face flushed a deep shade of red.

"Emma, don't make me come to you. I wouldn't like that," he said, before adding, "and neither would you."

The creaking came to a stop, and he heard the gentle brush of a dress sliding against the wood of the rocking horse as she shuffled off.

"Yes, Papa," she said.

Mr. Chapman's shadow crept over her slight frame as she approached.

"Yes. Come closer now."

She took two more steps.

"Don't be shy now. I'm your papa."

She took another step.

His rough hands curled around her tiny, white arms and pulled her in and up. She let out a gasp from the sudden movement before coming to land on his knee.

"There you go, Emma. That's much better, isn't it?" He looked into her eyes.

"Where are you now, Emma? Tell me where you're sitting," he asked, his eyes still looking into hers.

"I'm on your lap, Papa," her voice seemed even lighter than before, almost breaking on the vowels.

"Yes, you are. You're making Papa much happier now." He spoke to her with that peculiar voice adults use when they speak to children.

He bounced Emma on his knee, cradling her back with his left hand to stop her from falling and his right hand came to rest above her exposed knee.

"There we go, Emma. Just like the rocking horse. You can ride me like the rocking horse. Do you like that? You can lean forward and rest your hands on my other leg and pretend you're at a gallop."

She nodded but said no words. Her face turned away from him now, her eyes staring at the pattern sewn into the rug on the floor. She leaned forward and placed her hands on his knee. He repositioned them further up his leg.

Emma sniffed and a few tears fell from her eyes when she blinked and ran down the white skin of her arms, coming to rest at the bend in her wrist before falling inwards and out of sight.

Mr. Chapman continued, sliding his hand further down her back. He tugged at the bottom of her dress, pulling it up and out from under her, releasing a muffled moan as he pulled it free.

Emma continued to bounce while the man's hand disappeared under her dress.

Nicholas's throat tightened. Without another thought, he burst from the wardrobe, every ounce of his compact frame fixed on breaking every bone in that hand, but he didn't make it even a few steps beyond the door.

As Emma's skirt rose higher, exposing more of her thigh, it also revealed something else: a garter. Light reflected off something held against her leg.

And in one smooth motion, as Mr. Chapman's hands slid further beneath her, she reached down the side of her leg to grasp a thin knife hidden there. And it was when he closed his eyes and massaged his hand against her small body, that she drew the knife and slid it up and into his throat.

He didn't make a noise. In fact, he didn't even seem to notice at first. His body did, though. Dark blood poured down his neck and under and over his stained shirt. Emma pushed the knife deeper into Mr. Chapman with a firm grip, not letting go, her tiny voice rumbling deep inside her chest.

The bouncing stopped. A gurgling noise bubbled in his throat, ethereal, like it came from someone sitting behind him. Emma jumped off and stumbled back. Mr. Chapman reached for his neck and his fingers came to rest on the wooden handle of the utensil now lodged in his jugular. The cut was wide. Emma lodged the knife inside his throat with such a smooth, forceful motion that it pierced through the bottom of his mouth, the blade sticking itself between two of his molars.

The man's eyes frantically looked about the room he would die in and came to rest on Emma, his eyes more fearful than hers for the first time. He glanced at Nicholas, confused. He tried to speak but nothing came out save for a few incoherent grunts and, finally, a soul-deep sigh that rattled from his chest as his life left him and his eyes went blank. They didn't shut on his way to the floor. He landed with a heavy thud. The only noise left in the room came from the chests of two children, adrenaline racking every ounce of muscle between them.

Emma shook as she brought her hands up in front of her, streaked with the red stain of what she did. She cried and heaved and rubbed them against her dress, trying to remove the blood but it only spread further and smeared across her skin.

Nicholas didn't have a response for this. He knelt and placed his hand on her shoulder. She jumped at his touch, but in an instant, she closed the gap between them and wrapped her arms around his neck before burying her head into his chest. She sobbed into him.

He held his sister like this many times, comforting her for all manner of scrapes and sadness. His sister had never cried as hard as Emma did now, but his sister had never killed a man trying to rape her.

CHAPTER FORTY-SEVEN

NED WAS HOT AND WET, but he wasn't dead. He hurt everywhere. Something dug into his back. He squirmed, and a cramp seized his chest, making the tiny space he found himself in feel even smaller. The sweet, heady smell of wood ash filled his nostrils.

The bricks of a fireplace framed his view into a darkened room. Wet stockings hung above him, dripping onto his arms and legs.

"Aw, shite," he muttered.

Despite the pain in his sides and the pounding in his skull, he pulled himself out of the hearth with a few awkward motions.

"Ned?"

He was in Emma's room. She lay on the bed near him, her hair across her face. She was splayed out under the sheets, taking up the entire bed. The image caught him off guard and reminded him of his mother… when she was still sick, shaking under the worn sheets.

His breath caught in his throat. His mother. He remembered his mother.

"Ned?"

"Emma, I can see her. I see my mother. I see everything. Where

I grew up. My home, my bed." Tears were already streaming down his face, his mind overwhelmed as it chased down old memories like fresh moments.

She reached out to him, urging him to her.

"My memory. I have it all," he said, between sobs.

Emma sat up and pulled his head down to her lap.

Places and people Ned never met became old haunts and good friends. His brain grew hot as it rushed to fill in gaps so wide they'd never been crossed. He heard his own heartbeat, and then a second heartbeat. No, it was two other heartbeats.

He sat up and muttered something under his breath.

He placed his hand on Emma's stomach and yanked it back. "I don't, I think you're—"

"I'm what?" she asked, pulling the blankets over her naked body.

They stared at one another, neither wanting to be the first to speak anything into reality.

"How can you know that?" Emma asked.

"I don't know. I feel a heart beating. Not mine and not yours."

"Ned, I'm happy your memories have returned, but this… it's too much. I don't know how to respond to this."

"Let's start with this." Ned took her hand. "Are you happy?"

She turned away from him.

Ned's grip loosened. He sighed, "Neither of us planned for children, but—"

"I don't know how to love you, but I care what happens to you more than I do myself. That's the closest thing I can give you. I just—"

"I love you, too."

She shook her head. "Of course you do." She smirked, the half-smile fading as she stared back at him, her eyes glistening in the waning moonlight. "What kind of parents will we be? You're… changing." She sat up. Her leathers fell from the bed, clanking her knives against the floor. "And I'm not a mother. I don't even know my own parents."

"What does it matter?"

"It matters, Ned. If they were wretched, then my life makes sense. If they were kind and I still ended up with this life, then what's the point? I refuse to be responsible for the same horrors being inflicted on another child."

He brushed the hair from her face.

She flicked her head away from his hand. "Do you know who I am? Do you think I'm a good person, Ned?"

"No, I don't. There's no such thing as good or bad people. There are good decisions and bad decisions and the best thing we can ever be is something in between. Never too good, never too bad, we do enough to never be thought of as either. That's what I think we are. A collection of the best and worst decisions made by us and for us. Same as anybody else. And I think we've done well, considering."

She snorted.

"Look, I don't know who I am or why I see the things I see or can do the things I do, but I know that I can make my own path with them. It might sound silly to use these powers to help children instead of using it to become wealthy or to rule Scotland, but it excites me more than any of those alternatives. Every time I picture it, you're there."

Emma kissed him before bunching the blankets around her, covering herself.

They sat that way for some time. They laughed with each other, cried, imagined the future. A small candle on a nearby table flickered yellow shadows across the room as it melted into a puddle of itself. Emma stretched her bare legs out across Ned's lap.

"Do you always sleep naked?"

"Of course," she said.

"I thought you did that for me."

"You would." She kicked his arm. "Lie with me."

Ned placed his hat on the bedside table and stretched out beside her.

"I'm still not saying I believe you, but if you're right, what will we call our baby?" she asked.

"Anything but Ned."

She laughed, echoing him, "Anything but Ned."

"I can still feel it. Memories, they're forcing themselves into me. It's like thousands of drawers being added to my life. I still have to open them, but it's nice to know none of them are empty."

A sudden spasm brought his hands up to clutch the back of his head. The veins in his neck strained. Emma cradled him in her arms, squeezing him tight.

"I can see my mother again, the workshop. There's a young girl there with red hair. Samantha, I call her Sam. Oh, no…"

"What?"

"I have a sister—had a sister. She passed, so did my mum. I missed her funeral, but I can see her grave. It's near my childhood home. I wonder if it still stands?"

He cycled between sobbing and choking on laughter, his mind racked with joy and pain in equal measure. "I worked in a coal mine. I can't stop it. I hear voices I've never heard, but they're friends. I can see my…"

"See what, Ned?"

"I can see my father."

"James? What was he like then?"

"It's… not James."

"What do you mean it's not James?"

"He looks nothing like James." Ned sat up straight. "Where is he?"

"He's in the room across the hall."

Ned struggled to his feet before bolting to James's door, pounding his fist into it.

"James, I need to speak with you!" he shouted. He slammed his fist again. "James!"

There was a muffled scream from behind.

"Quiet now, Ned. You'll wake the other guests," James said, a coolness to his words not present before.

James stood behind Emma, his hand over her mouth. Ned rushed back through the door.

"No closer!" James twisted his other hand, and the rising sun caught the flat side of a small dagger as he pointed at Emma's belly.

"Who are you?" Ned asked.

"You still don't know who I am? I suppose I have aged poorly. Ned, look at my face. Look at my eyes."

Dawn approached and light skipped the cracks in James's face, forcing the dark to huddle in wrinkles around his eyes, mouth, and forehead. James pulled the knife away from Emma and slid it under Ned's hat. He raised it from the table and let it fall onto his own head.

"How about now?" James asked.

"You're..."

"Almost there."

"Me."

James smiled.

Emma struggled to free herself, but James held her close against him with no effort at all.

"Let her go."

"No, I won't do that. See, at first I worried she wouldn't be enough to force you to do what I need you to do. Now that she carries your child, well, I don't believe motivation will be an issue. Also, I just like pressing her body against mine. I can see why we like her. It's a shame about all this... damage," he said, dragging the tip of the dagger across her scarred flesh before letting it fall from her belly button down to the hair between her legs. "I haven't decided if I'm going to do anything else to her. One thing at a time. Also, let's do away with these names. I'm Nicholas. You're Nicholas. It's a pleasure to meet you."

Ned slammed his fist on the wall next to him. "We are not the same. I'm nothing like you."

"You are though. There's no sense wasting time on that." James traced the underside of one of Emma's breasts. "Can you feel that, my dear?"

Emma breathed heavily, not crying, but seething.

"Oh, not the knife. Of course you can feel that. I meant me. Can you feel me? The more you squirm, the more excited I get." He leaned closer to her ear and whispered, "I can't help it."

"What do you want?" Ned asked, his fists clenched.

"I need a heart, of a sort. It's in the workshop. There's a crystal in the centre of that ridiculous machine. You'll remember it now. I need you to bring it to me."

"Why?" Ned asked.

James rolled his eyes. He flicked his wrist and a thin red line appeared below Emma's right breast. "It doesn't matter why. Do it or I kill her, do it or I rape her, do it or I cut the fetus from her belly. Whatever horror is worse to you, that's the one I'll do. That is your why."

"Then you'll leave us."

Another flick of James's wrist and a second red cut appeared. This one deeper, a thin stream of blood ran from it like crimson tentacles.

"Stop! No more. I'll do it."

"Be quick. There's no telling what I can do in a few seconds."

CHAPTER FORTY-EIGHT

"WHO ARE YOU?" Emma asked, her voice muffled by her own sobs.

"Nicholas."

"What are you doing here?"

"I was hiding."

Emma glanced at the body beside them. Blood seeped into the rug under his wound, turning the lighter areas of the pattern as dark as the rest with a burnt copper tinge.

"I killed him." She brought her knees up to her chin and squeezed her arms around them. "The master, he'll kill me."

Her eyes were mad with fright. Nicholas took a loose sheet from the bed and threw it across the body. It settled over the man, removing the gruesome image from view.

Emma buried her face in her arms; she whispered the same words over and over. She looked up, her face wet with tears, thick makeup stained her cheeks.

"Emma, it's okay now. You're safe," he said.

"I'm not safe. I'm going to die. He'll never let me live."

He knelt beside her, coming between her and the body.

"Emma?"

She shook her head and her eyes came into focus on Nicholas's face. She pushed her dark hair behind one of her ears with a shaking hand and pulled her dress down and straightened it around her knees.

"Why were you hiding?" she asked.

"I'm looking for a friend. I have this thing," he paused, showing her the metallic flower. "It led me here."

"That led you here?" she asked, reaching for it. She rolled it around in her stained hands. The bulb sparked but she didn't react.

"It's hard to explain. It finds things, people too. You think about them and it leads you there."

She raised an eyebrow. "What's her name? Your friend."

"Sam. She has red hair—"

"You mean Samantha?"

"Yes, Samantha."

"She's the master's."

"Who's the master?"

"They, the other men, they call him the Dollmaker. He makes us… he's taking her with him."

"Sam? Where is he taking her?" he asked.

"I–I don't…" she trailed off.

"Emma, please. If this is happening to her…" he swallowed hard, realising this same nightmare could very well be happening to his friend. "I have to help her."

"He moves girls to different countries all the time. Men like him," she said, looking at the sheet at the foot of the bed, "are everywhere."

"I have to find her," he said, looking around the room as if he expected to find a clue to her whereabouts.

"It's too late," Emma said.

"It's not too late. I can find her."

"No, I mean, it's too late for you." Emma rose to her feet and slipped the metallic flower into a pocket on her dress, a curious look in her eyes.

"What do you mean?" he asked.

She took several steps backward. Her fright now gone, replaced with some sort of anticipation or nervousness, he couldn't tell which.

"Emma?"

As she reached the door, she grasped the handle behind her back, her eyes never leaving him.

"I'm sorry." She frowned. "I'm so sorry. They'll kill me. They'll kill me if they find me here with him like this."

"What are you doing? We'll find a way—"

Emma screamed.

She opened the door. "Run. I'm sorry. You have to run."

And then she screamed again.

He flinched and the weight of what she did hit him as unexpectedly as the knife she slid into the man's throat.

And he ran.

CHAPTER FORTY-NINE

NED APPEARED IN THE WORKSHOP. His mind fluid now; he could feel everything, everyone, at once. Entering the workshop was as simple as thinking about it. Staying here took no effort at all; no more than he needed to tell his brain to breathe. He had lived an entire life with these powers, and now both his body and mind knew it too.

A black desk sat in front of him. A green-lamped light and a plaque lay on its surface.

"It seems I only ever see this place in a hurry now," Ned said aloud.

A voice broke the silence. "You talk to yourself. We aren't so different after all." A man stepped from a darkened corner of the room. As the shadow slid from his face, he recognized the voice immediately.

"James? You said you couldn't be here!"

The man raised his hands. "This is going to be difficult for you, but I am not the man you know as James."

Ned moved with a ferocity that caught the stranger off guard. Displaying a growing mastery of his powers. He lifted the stranger off the ground and threw him down on the table, his hands gripped around his neck.

"Wait! Please..." the man gasped. "Use your gifts, search my heart, it's the same."

He was right. Ned knew before he even dove at him. This wasn't James. He released him.

"I'm so sick of your face. I'm done with these games." This wasn't the same man holding Emma in Inverness, but he still sensed a darkness in him. "You aren't him, but we are not the same."

"That's true." The stranger caught his breath, pushing himself up and off the table. "I'm a far worse version of you."

Ned pointed towards the glowing crystal in the heart of the machine. "I need that, and I don't care who you are."

"Please, hear me out. You needn't worry about Emma. Only a handful of seconds will pass while you are here."

"Having met two versions of myself, I'm starting to not like me very much."

"I don't blame you, but please. Just a moment."

Ned glanced at the writing on the table. "What do you want?"

"Not that," Nicholas said, pointing at the crystal. "I don't want that. It's what he wants, and I know you're trying to think of a way to make sure he doesn't get it."

"Aye," Ned replied. "Do you have an idea?"

"Not an idea, just advice. You should let him have it."

Ned pulled the chair away from the desk and sat down. "Ah, so you're the version of me that rolls over and accepts his fate?"

"No, I'm not a version of you at all, "Nicholas said, pacing around his younger self. "You're a version of me. I'm the first of us. Nicholas Locherbie."

"That would explain why you look so old then," Ned jabbed.

"Will you let me help you?"

Ned motioned for Nicholas to sit.

"I will make this as brief as I can. Right now, James exists in between worlds. He is strong enough to exist in your timeline, but not completely. He needs the heart of the workshop to take this place from you. Once he has it, he will leave your world and enter mine. Well, what's left of mine. He will be stronger than any of us who have come before, and he will continue to consume. He is an embodiment of my own unrestrained ambition."

"Unrestrained ambition. And you want me to give him the heart?" Ned asked.

"Aye, what he hasn't considered, I hope, is that once he absorbs it, he will become permanent in your timeline, for a time, which also means—"

"He'll be vulnerable."

Nicholas wanted to smile with pride but knew the moment didn't call for it.

"Right now, he is never completely in one place, so even if we were to kill him in Inverness or I somehow killed him in the void where he exists with me, it would not be complete. But once he takes control of your workshop, he will be tied to that timeline until he attempts to move to the next."

"So, he absorbs the heart and I run him through with a sword?"

"Perhaps Emma would be more reliable, but yes, that's the idea."

"I'd take offence, but I know you're right." He ran a finger along the edge of the table's engraving. "What a waste. What a waste of all this power."

"It's not a complete waste. Not yet."

A dozen corporeal bodies emerged from the darkness of the workshop, pulled from the edges. Some shone with a brilliant golden light. Others moved as white smoke, passing through and around objects in their path. Still others walked with an eerie blue glow, their movement slow and somehow comforting. The lamp trembled as they approached.

Ned stood. "Who are they?" he asked.

"These are those who came before us. Some of them. These are the only ones you'd wish to meet, anyway."

The ghosts were still, each facing Ned, their eyes unmoving.

"Our gifts come with a decision. You may do whatever you wish with them. Some of us choose to do ill, like James," he paused, "or myself."

"What did you do?" Ned asked.

Nicholas grimaced. "I lost people close to me and I tried to bring them back."

"That doesn't sound terrible. Tell me the truth."

"You cannot bring someone back, but that didn't stop me from trying. I did things, unholy things, to see them again. I worked against nature and others paid dearly for it."

The ghosts surrounding them flickered and phased out of sight.

"Then I made it worse."

"How?" Ned leaned in.

Nicholas shook his head. "How do I explain this? To you, of all people. I tried to change the past, or I thought I did. Normally, when people like us pass from this life, we join the workshop to aid the next in line, a son or daughter. Our duty is to contribute to the development and success of the next, but we are also given the gift to experience our life again, move through events like chapters in a book, constrained to our own timeline, separate from reality, but exact in every detail. We are not active participants though, only viewers. We cannot change the outcomes. It's limitless nostalgia.

"I broke it, though. I discovered a way to influence myself as a child."

"The voice in my head. That was you?"

"Aye. I wanted a different ending. A better one. And since I was the first of our kind without an heir, my power grew as I aged. I thought if I made different decisions as a child, I would live a better life. I would not fill my memories with death and mistakes, but my family and friends would live."

"You tried to save them by erasing the man you would become and—"

"In doing so, created you."

"And James."

"And James. Right now, all his actions have no implication on reality. All of this is taking place in a pocket, closed off from the real world. If that were all he could impact, I might walk away, comfortable knowing that he would erase everything created because of my foolish attempts to better my past.

"Unfortunately, he is more powerful than any of us. I didn't account for his ability to absorb the heart of the workshop in other timelines. If he gains enough power, he can leave this theatre and enter reality."

Ned buried his head in his hands.

"You have a courage I never had. You are so much of who I wanted to be. I never thought it possible."

"Who did you want to be?"

Nicholas straightened, surprised. "I wanted to be like my—our—father. And you are more like him than I ever was."

"My father? It's been so long since we've spoken. In fact, it was here, in this place." Ned said, still surprised at his ability to recall. "Has he shown himself to you?"

Nicholas shook his head.

Ned did not linger on this note, growing eager to return to Emma. "Can't you go back along your own timeline, stop yourself from adjusting it?"

"I could, but James can affect the timeline directly. Anything I whisper to my younger self can be immediately, and physically, altered by him as long as he is between worlds. He's done it already, several times."

"When?"

"I'm not the only voice in your head. He's spoken to you, contradicting me. He's appeared to you in different forms in order to direct you. He's even brought people you know from other timelines into yours."

Realisation spread across Ned's face. He breathed deep.

"So, I give him the heart, he absorbs it, and I run a sword through him."

"Well, again, it might be better if Emma—"

"I'm not useless with a sword, man."

"Your intentions might be known to him before you act. Emma's less so. He can move at the spark of a thought, and he is more comfortable with his powers than you are. If you fail—"

"I won't fail. If I can rid this world of him and create a new one, a better one, I won't fail."

"I hope so."

"You don't trust me to do it?" Ned asked.

"I trust you," Nicholas said.

Ned pulled the heart from its resting place. The amber lights along the walls flickered and then died, leaving them in a colourless grey. The only light remaining came from the ghosts shifting around him, casting shadows that warped the dimensions of the room.

"I have one question before I leave, but I'm scared to say it aloud," Ned said.

"Ask it."

"If all of this is happening in a timeline separate from reality," Ned paused, afraid to say the words, "I don't exist, do I? I'm just a new branch on a family tree that's locked away from the real one."

Nicholas cleared his throat. "I'm afraid so."

"It's a shame." Ned chuckled, staring into the heart of the workshop. "For the first time in my life, I feel real."

"I know." Nicholas sighed. "If it makes you feel better, you're very real to me."

Ned pulled his gaze from the swirling liquid inside the crystal and glanced at Nicholas. "It doesn't," he said, then vanished.

CHAPTER FIFTY

Nicholas felt older than he ever had. Ned's presence had warmed him, but he was alone now. The spectres flickered in and out around him, all of them having grown silent to him long ago. Still, he felt different, uneasy. He stared into the darkest corner of the workshop and saw nothing but displaced shadows moved about by gloom and imagination.

Then he felt it. Memories forming inside his mind of his conversation with Ned, but from a perspective not his own. He could simultaneously remember speaking with Ned, but could also see himself speaking with Ned.

Another figure, small and distant grew on the horizon of his mind, away from the noise of life, away from the silence of death, festering in a small seam in his own mind.

Laughter erupted all around him. A sound he hadn't heard in years. Then out from the nothing, his quarry stepped.

The man who stood before him reflected him perfectly. Not like Ned, but of himself as he was now, old and bent, grey and weak.

"Hello, Nicholas," the doppelgänger said, his words thick with sweet and rot.

CHAPTER FIFTY-ONE

The hallway seemed longer than before and with each step, a door swung open along its length, its tenants alerted by Emma's screams. Several girls entered the hall from their rooms. They were all identical, wearing the same style of dress in a different shade of pastel, their hair pulled into the same ponytails tied with matching ribbon.

Men stumbled out after them in various states of dress. The kitchen help gathered in the opposite hallway. Nicholas saw several men hanging over the railing on the second floor above the main entrance, looking for the source of the disturbance.

The Dollmaker appeared at the top of the stairs, his shirt unbuttoned, mouth reddened by smeared lipstick, clutching a green dress in his hands.

Then Emma appeared from the hallway. Her arms were covered in blood, now dry. She screamed again, hysterical and panicked, and brought her hand up to point at him.

"He killed him!" she screamed.

That put the whole second floor into motion. The Dollmaker

shouted at several men who were already charging down the stairs.

Nicholas burst from the building and stumbled through the narrow closes. He ran smack into walls at each turn, moving too fast to adjust. The men in pursuit shouted after him. Looking ahead, he saw his exit to High Street. Blurry shadows passed by the opening as he got closer, and his eyes adjusted to the extra light.

There was only one safe place, so he turned west towards the workshop. He bumped into several people trying to get around them and spun out of the way of a slow-moving wagon. Every so often, he risked a glance back to confirm there were still men pursuing him. The crowds were dense and difficult to squeeze through, but seemed to part with ease for the large group stampeding after him.

The pain in his knees was excruciating. Bone grinded against bone, the smooth articulation of a simple step replaced by something more mechanical, more clumsy.

Still, he made it back to Lady Stair's Close. His lungs were burning, but the state of Makar's Court concerned him more. Massive crates and wagons were spread out across the space, storage for performers preparing for an evening festival.

Several wooden boxes covered the workshop's trap door. He slammed against the one closest to him. It didn't budge. Hiding wasn't an option. There were too many people and blockades covered the other exits.

Nicholas raced to a nearby ladder that reached to the roof of the building.

Up.

His heart sank. Could he even climb in his condition? Nicholas followed the instruction. He ran to the ladder and, wrapping his fingers around a rung, pulled himself up one step at a time. It was slow, and when he reached the second floor of the building, he heard shouts from below. His pursuers pooled beneath him. There were at least five of them now. They demanded he come down, promising they wouldn't hurt him.

Keep climbing.

Just before reaching the top, the men shook the ladder, taunting him. Nicholas gripped the rungs. He wasn't coming down and the group must have realised this as they climbed up after him.

They were fast. He rolled from the ladder and to his feet. The roof was barren of anything but dirt, dust, and a lone chimney stack.

He ran to it, hid behind the bricks. His lungs heaved. Could he slide down the chimney? No, he'd get stuck or die from the fall.

"Where are ya, lad?" The men reached the roof.

"Come on now, we aren't ginna hurtcha," the other one said.

"The Dollmaker might," the first one said with a wheezy laugh.

Jump, Nicholas.

He stepped out from behind the chimney.

"That's it, now." One man extended his hand towards Nicholas.

He looked at it, then looked to his right. He spotted a building he might reach if he ran hard enough.

Without another option, he summoned all his energy for his first few steps. The quick shouts from the men became noise and everything else blurred into a wall of colour that seemed to wrap itself around a singular point of focus—the gap he needed to clear.

He would make it.

He'd jumped this far before.

The muscles in his legs screamed as his old injuries inflamed, but he pushed the building away and launched his body into the air. His limbs flailed about like windmills and the air rushed against his face as the other building lurched closer, as if to catch him.

He felt weightless for a brief sliver of time. As he reached the height of his jump, he saw all of Scotland stretch out in front of him. From where he was, frozen in mid-air, he could see all the way to the top of Arthur's Seat.

Then the wind in his face changed direction. It began rushing up from beneath him. His limbs stopped flailing, and he crashed onto the flat stone of the building opposite. He tumbled forward and tripped, skinning his arm. Adrenaline eclipsed the pain pulsing through his body. He jumped to his feet and looked back. The men shouted at him, before he disappeared down another ladder to the street below, lost to them forever.

CHAPTER FIFTY-TWO

"So, you decided to show yourself," Nicholas said to the intruder.

"I'm paying my respects to the dead," James said.

"You're both here and there. Incredible." Nicholas said, failing to hide his awe.

"Did you think there would be no consequence for your actions? Whispering in your own ear like that."

"Honestly, no. I don't excel at thinking ahead."

"I mean, you might have been able to revise your life into something better in this ghastly charade of ours, but I've been making some changes of my own. A small choice here, a small choice there, a doctor intended to be in a hamlet to save a mother here, gets called away to help those trapped in a cave-in there—"

"You're a monster," Nicholas said.

The imposter clapped his hands together with glee.

"And what of all the others who died in that mine just so you could spare your father this time around? You took an accident that took dozens of lives and passed your pain onto someone else.

You are as selfish and as cruel as you ever were. It's impressive. It's the only part of you I like."

A tremble rushed into Nicholas, as if the space they occupied fractured. He grew weak. "How are you doing this? How could you hide from me in my own memories?"

"Have you seen yourself? You're broken. The hard part wasn't hiding from you. There are enough cracks in that mind of yours to hide more than me. The question you should be asking yourself is—"

"How did you enter my memories?" Nicholas interrupted. "You spoke to him, to us, as a boy."

"That's the one," his copy breathed in, savouring the moment. "While you were making slight adjustments to your life as a boy, the new choices he made created small pockets where alternative futures festered, not quite their own distinct realities, more like frayed threads on the edge of a quilt. What you didn't realise because of your obsessive and moronic pursuit of penitence is that, unlike all that have come before you, your actions here, in this place, have weight. Do you know why?"

Nicholas swallowed. "I have no children."

"Precisely. Every single one of us passed their control on when the time came, begrudgingly or not. Instead, you kept yours. You never had a child, and you choked the life from this place. So, I find you here, grey and spent, still clutching to the one thing that made you special, albeit weaker." James ran a hand through his thinning hair. "Even this place ages."

"If you're like me, you know how this ends. Why continue? Why not try something different?"

"Because you're already doing that." James leaned in close to Nicholas and whispered, "I'm the version of you that sees his actions to the end."

Nicholas stepped back.

"Every time one of your decisions created one of these aborted alternatives, I was there. They were malformed and so I could enter at will, do what I pleased. I've ripped out the heart of the workshop so many times I've lost count. They weren't satisfying, but they were enough to allow me to move in and out of this world, not just speak to it like you do."

"No," the word was almost inaudible. As all of Ned's memories slid through his mind, he realised that with Ned's first use of the workshop, the gap between Nicholas as a boy and Ned had been bridged. He collapsed.

"Fortunately, time is not linear. For us, anyway. You gave Nicholas a new beginning which requires a new ending. Time fills in the middle gap last, which is why you saw none of this coming and why poor Ned can't remember his childhood. The two halves of his life weren't connected yet. This allowed me to enter your new childhood and plant your powers, of which I possess several times as much as you. I put them into people we met as a child, then jumped ahead and led Ned to each one. Our powers are outside of time, even if the carriers are not.

"That doesn't explain the victims. Why does Ned gain his power through death? That's never how it happens!"

"To be honest, I didn't know they would die when they handed them back, but they are weak shells, aren't they?"

"How dare you speak of them like toys!"

"Hypocrite."

A hand came to rest on the back of Nicholas's head and in an instant, he tumbled to the stones of Edinburgh's Makar Court. He hadn't returned to his present in a very long time. The city burned. The entire sky filled with amber light. Staring at it caused him to go mad. Its source, the workshop, pulsed beneath the city, threatening to implode.

"No, go back. Go back before it ends!" He tried to wrestle himself from his copy's grip.

"Have you told any of them that you aren't actually dead? That you ran from the world to save yourself while the world awaited its fate, frozen in amber until the moment you're ready to let them die? Not a few, old man. All of them."

Nicholas sobbed into the stone.

"Please, please don't let it end."

The world faded and froze in place as he returned to the void.

He stood, faced himself. "We aren't fit for this power."

"We are as fit as any. More so. I have seen things you haven't. I've gone back to the beginning of us hundreds of times. We are all such terrible children," his reflection said.

"We cannot all be cruel."

"Of course not, but most of us are. What does that tell you of man, when given the choice, we more often than not choose darkness? Is that a design flaw or destiny?"

Nicholas sat, defeated. "It's a choice like any other. I know that to be true because I've made them both."

"You did not make a choice. You were corrupt then and you are corrupt now. You just went soft. I'm here to see it through."

"You're the devil."

"If there is a devil, Nicholas. We are surely him."

CHAPTER FIFTY-THREE

NED RETURNED ONLY moments after he left, the heart clutched in his hand so tight it threatened to break.

"That took you a little longer than I expected," James said, both him and Emma still in the same position Ned left them in. "Place it on the bed."

"Release her."

"Why would I do that? She's three times as dangerous as you are, even with your gifts. Place the heart on the bed or I'm going to keep cutting things."

Ned relented and tossed it onto the bed.

James nudged Emma forward, keeping her in front of him while he reached for the amber crystal. He found it amongst the tousled sheets and held it up to the limited light piercing the window shade.

"This is where we part ways, I'm afraid. Enjoy your remaining time together. It won't be long until none of you exist at all."

James squeezed the heart of the workshop in one hand, tiny cracks appearing along its surface. He let his blade hand relax and as the amber light spilled through tiny ruptures, Ned spotted James's attention taken by the heart.

He let his hand fall to his side, the pad of his thumb finding his sword leaning against the wall. Just as his fingers gripped the hilt, he realised he wasn't the only one who saw James falter.

"Emma, no!" He rushed towards her.

Too late.

Emma leaned forward and whipped her head back, smashing the crystal into James's face. His nose exploded with a spatter of blood. The heart came loose from his grip and shattered across the floor, amber liquid coating the wood, mixing with blood.

Without pausing, she lunged towards her knives, pulled two of them and had them buried in James's neck and chest before he knew she'd escaped his grasp.

James stood stunned, his body failing him. He stumbled back into the wall, using it to support his weight. He bled out and the daggers, tipped with poison, acted fast.

Even as life left him, he wore a sickly smirk on his face, his eyes locked on Ned. No, not on Ned. Behind Ned.

He turned to follow his gaze. Emma lay propped up against the far wall. Slices of morning sunlight crossed her body and, for a moment, even in this state, she felt as much a part of this room as any other. Then his eyes moved to her stomach, and the sight struck him.

There was a dagger deep inside her.

"No, no, no, no, Emma. Emma, lie down."

She wasn't even aware of it. She looked up at him, confused. "Why is he smiling?" Emma asked. "Ned, why is he—"

She stopped as the pain caught up to her. Ned rushed to her, and she crumpled into him.

"The knife, the knife. The baby. Ned, please don't let it hurt the baby."

"Keep breathing, focus on my face. The baby will be fine."

James slid to the ground. "You... were too... hasty," he

sputtered, blood pouring from his lips. He died, but his face held the maniacal expression.

"Is he dead? Ned, is he dead?" Emma squeezed his arms, her grip loosening and tightening as if her heartbeat was inside her palms.

Ned was defeated, the plan having failed. He stared down at Emma, her eyes showing fear for the first time since they met in the Dollmaker's mansion so long ago. She clung to him again, broken in a different way. This time, he broke with her and, through tears, nodded. "He's dead." Kissing her forehead, he repeated, "He's dead. You did good, love."

Emma smiled, but the recognition of what was happening inside her wiped it away.

A heavy weight formed in Ned's heart. One he didn't think he'd known before, but had. Too many times, in fact.

She hadn't killed James, only delayed him. This truth plagued his thoughts while he tried to make sense of the scene. He squeezed Emma, but she didn't squeeze back. The only woman he ever loved lay still beside him.

CHAPTER FIFTY-FOUR

Nicholas stood alone. A few glimmers from wandering spectres lit dark corners, but the workshop light dimmed on the edge of his mind. One final thought nagged him—no matter what he did, he could save none of them. He couldn't avoid disaster. He existed now as a man outside of time, without a home, left with only the whispers of tortured sounds.

He had one last message to deliver. The one he should have started with.

CHAPTER FIFTY-FIVE

NICHOLAS FOUND a small rock next to his foot and tossed it up, trying to catch it in the dark. It thudded into the dirt with every miss until, finally, he caught it. The stone slapped against the pad of his hand. He caught it three more times in a row. He tried for a fifth consecutive catch, a world record, no doubt. It fell into his hand at the same moment a loud crack, crunch, and a rumble echoed nearby. He moved closer to the gate and felt a tremor from the other side.

The noise grew, then a flurry of pounding caused him to jerk his head away. He scrambled to the dirt and found the rope, gripped it tight and yanked, throwing himself back at the same time.

Cailean burst through, his lantern flooding the shaft just in time for Nicholas to see the roof of the tunnel collapse.

Save him.

Nicholas reacted to the words out of instinct. He reached for Cailean, searching for his hands, anything to pull him forward. He found the rope and yanked on it. Cailean flew past Nicholas and into the open area past the door. The momentum caused Nicholas to stumble forward. Their positions now switched. Cailean screamed to Nicholas to get out of the tunnel, but it was too late. As if the sound from his small lungs split it, the rock above Nicholas came down on top of him, the light of the lantern extinguished at the same time.

NICHOLAS'S EYES BLINKED OPEN. The world remained dark, refusing to come into focus.

He couldn't feel his arms or legs, but he knew they were there. He grew warm as blood pooled beneath his tiny body, each breath shallow and repetitive as he only took in enough air to get him to the next.

His eyes strained to search the darkness so hard they felt as if they might burst from their sockets.

Pain overtook the shock. It hurt to breathe.

Nicholas didn't have a grand vision then, and he did not leave the world with eloquent words. A series of small, rapid breaths were all that left his lips before the blood seeped into his lungs.

He counted each breath as he died.

NICHOLAS WATCHED as the younger version of himself lay in the dark, alone and afraid. His own mind felt loose and fractured, fuzzy even, as he witnessed the result of his actions. He knelt beside the boy, wanted to comfort him, but could not.

"Time is irrelevant in the moment before you leave this world, isn't it?"

He lay on his side now, along the length of his younger self, their breathing taking on the same shallow rhythm.

"We all live three lives: a sojourn in the dark, warm molasses of the womb, a blink and a breath that is our walk on this earth, and an eternity in the seconds before it all goes dark."

He felt a tremor but could no longer know if it came from outside him or inside him. Was it a memory forming or slipping away? Did he make the good choice or the cowards choice? Did he save them all or just himself? Did he end something or start something anew?

He did not remember, and then, after a few more breaths left his lungs, could not remember.

CHAPTER FIFTY-SIX

NED LAY Emma across the workshop table. Moments earlier, he wasn't even sure he could bring her to this place. Now he had his mind made up to use it to save her.

He pulled back the sheet he wrapped her in, exposing the wound. The blade was inside her, up to the hilt. It was only now he noticed which knife James used. He tapped a finger to the tip of the hilt and it popped open, amber dust sparkling around the opening.

He pressed his ear to Emma's mouth. There was warmth. Her breath was caught in time, moistening the air above her lips. Blood had almost ceased pouring from her stomach, but even here, with time nearly frozen, it continued to drip from the table to the floor with sickly repetition. Ned scrambled to the opening in the table and froze. He didn't know what to do. He raised his hands, but nothing came to him. The sizzle never rose up his spine as it did as a child. His hands shook. He wiped his palms on his pants and warmed them over her body like any of his creations. Nothing.

"No, no, no, please. Please work. Please do something."

He rested a hand on her head, the other on her stomach. A thin connection. His left hand was drawn to his right, but it was only their proximity, nothing else.

"Help me!" Ned screamed at the ghosts. "What good are you if all you do is show me how to make trinkets? Help me save her!"

He buckled, his face dropping to Emma's still body.

"You shouldn't have brought her here, Nicholas."

Ned's head rose, the hair on the back of his neck standing on end. He felt the rush of memory flood through him, and he choked back tears at the sight of the man standing in front of him.

"Father?"

The large man nodded.

"Help me."

"I'm sorry. There's nothing I can do, son."

"What good is any of this!" He threw loose scraps of metal and leather into the corner.

"We aren't gods, Nicholas. We're whispers with a few tricks."

"No, he told me to save her. When I was a child, I—he told me to save Mother. He must have known a way."

"That wasn't him. That was the one you know as James. He was manipulating you to create a pull to the workshop. It worked."

"I'll take her to a doctor. I can be there in an instant."

Ned slid his hands under Emma's neck and knees, preparing to leave the workshop, when he felt his father's hand on his arm.

He recoiled. "You… can touch me?"

"Son, you can't go back."

"How are you able to touch me now?"

"You can't go back anymore. He's ended it. Nicholas ended his and your life to stop James. I'm sorry, son."

"What are you saying?"

"I'm saying the moment you step outside this workshop, you cease to exist. Emma will live. The only reason she's here now is because of that dagger. It's holding her here. If you remove the knife, she'll be wherever her life took her had she not met you."

"How did—"

"The cave-in. You didn't make it out this time."

"Then how am I still here?"

"You slipped inside the workshop before it happened."

"But if I'm stuck here and I can speak to you, touch you, does that mean—"

"I'm so sorry. You've joined the workshop, like me, like all of us here. When I said you shouldn't have brought her, I meant you shouldn't have brought your child here."

Ned looked back at Emma.

"When a child enters the workshop, the process starts again."

Ned stumbled back in shock. "I did it to you and now I've done it to myself."

His father wrapped his arm around him, pulling him close. "It's okay, son."

Pressed against his father's chest, Ned felt something release inside both of them and come loose. He cried as his mind clung to a moment only minutes before, when he had everything he ever wanted, a life before and a life after. Now he had only a life before, something he would have given anything for only a few days earlier.

"What do I do?"

"You let them go. You remove the knife."

"If I send Emma back, she will be as if I never met her."

"Aye."

"That would erase the child inside her. I can't."

"Nicholas, you're robbing her of her life, even if it is without you."

"I'm trying to give her the life she wants! The life we want!"

"And you think you know the life she wants?"

"Of course I do! How could you say that? How could—you don't know her. You don't even know me. Why am I listening to you?" Ned broke away and leaned against the table.

"Nicholas..."

"That name! It makes me sick to hear it. I know it's mine, but I don't hear myself in it any more than I do with Ned or James. They're just letters and sounds. Nothing feels real to me."

"I never told you of your namesake. An error in judgement. Another mystery I wanted to save until you were older, when we discovered this place together."

"Well, here we are." Ned huffed.

"Your mother and I named you after the first of our kind—St. Nicholas of Myra."

Ned's eyes fixed to his father's. "You mean..."

His father nodded and dared a smile.

"So, I'm...and you?"

"We don't all end up filling the role. Your grandfather didn't. I only did for a time. Some of us, like your original self, use their gifts for selfish gains. It's not an easy calling and most of us are not equipped to handle it.

"This is why belief in us is so sporadic. Some generations believe in us because we are very real to them. They see us. They feel us. We bring a certain and specific joy. Other generations are skipped entirely and the world's belief in us wanes until another comes along to fulfil the duty."

Ned shook his head, struggling to process what he was hearing. "Why are you telling me this? I have a life I want to live. I don't need you to confuse me with childish myths."

"Not myths, Nicholas. I've done nothing but tell you the truth. You don't have to live the life I offer, but you cannot live this one either. You must send her back."

Ned stared through his father, his mind elsewhere, devising a plan. "Nicholas spoke to himself as a child. That means I can do the same. I could save myself from the cave-in, then save Emma from James, which would save me and our child."

"No, Nicholas could do this because he still had dominion over this place. He was childless. Even then, it was only within his own timeline, separate from that of the real world. You are not in control here and your child is unborn. Your only decision now is when, not if, you will release her."

Ned held Emma's hand, rubbed it against his cheek.

"The lineage ends with me, then. If I send her back, our child will not live. Emma will never meet me because I die as a child."

His father nodded.

"And what will I do here? The man who died as a child. I have no life to relive like the rest of you. All of you had real lives. You had families, friends, people you can revisit. You could all get drunk on nostalgia. I have nothing! All my memories are forfeit, everything I did meaningless."

His father stepped towards him, placing his hand on his shoulder. "That's not true. You have me," he paused as he reached into a red velvet pouch hanging from his belt, "and you have this."

From inside the bag, his father produced a glass dome fixed to a wooden base. Inside, all of Edinburgh, other places too that he couldn't name. Snow appeared to swirl inside the dome any time his father shook the bauble.

"What is it?"

"Do you remember our march to the coal mine every morning?"

"Aye."

"It hurt me every day to bring you to that place. I told myself we had no choice. We wouldn't have survived the winters without the little extra you brought in. It was never worth you losing your childhood though, certainly not worth your life. I could never give you the childhood I wanted you to have, and never used the workshop as often as those before me, but I did create something no one else did."

Ned's brow furrowed. "What is it?"

"It's a single day."

Ned reached for it.

"Careful. If it were to break here, I do not know what would happen."

"I won't let it fall."

Ned held the dome in his hand, the wooden base exquisite, the snow inside glinting amber from an unseen light source.

"Is this the entire world?"

"Aye. The whole thing. For you. A single day to do anything you wish, define it how you wish. One day to live in for eternity. It's not a lifetime, but it's the best I could do."

Ned lost himself in the magic held in his hands. His father's words swirling around him like the snow inside the glass globe.

"Thank you." He looked up at his father. "I don't deserve this."

"No, but I worked my entire life to give you this. Not because you deserve it, but because I do. I deserve to see my son happy in the end. It's yours, but first, you must let Emma go," his father pleaded.

"Can you join me? Here, inside this?"

"Aye, if that is how you want to spend your day. I will join you."

Ned nodded through tears. "It is."

He wept as he took Emma in for the last time, but waited until he could take unbroken breaths before wrapping his fingers around the hilt of the dagger.

He leaned in and whispered a few words in her ear.

Then he pulled the dagger from her.

CHAPTER FIFTY-SEVEN

SAMANTHA ROLLED a cornflower between her finger and thumb. She sat against the large tree that stretched out over the grave markers for her hamlet. Her dress was filthy. It wouldn't stop raining, but there was a dry patch where she sat. Still, her mother would yell at her when she returned home.

Sheep bleated from somewhere below the hill, breaking the moment of quiet she enjoyed. Not even the wind bothered her today. It was her, and her friend, the patter of rain against the green leaves above her, the splash of water against the stone markers across from her.

She slid the cornflower behind her ear and tightened her dress around her knees.

Words came to her, but her voice caught in her throat.

The sun broke through the clouds just above the horizon and the sky took on a reddish hue for a moment before navy clouds slid across again.

Samantha continued for another hour as the sun dwindled and flames came alive in the hamlet below. She spoke silent words with her friend, not about anything important but only of everything that mattered.

CHAPTER FIFTY-EIGHT

There is only one way to save a thing—you give it time.

Mr. Locherbie's thoughts sat heavy in the cradle of his mind as he poked at a yellow, crystalline ornament hanging from the Christmas tree. He tapped the amber bauble again; it swung with unexpected momentum as its string tangled and untangled, sending prismatic spots twirling around the room.

The surrounding walls appeared to shift, moved by shadows created by the slow flames of candles resting throughout the tree. Their glow lit the foil and glass of ornaments, casting him in flickering hues. He sifted the light between his fingers, admiring the change in tone.

The sweet scent of cooking meat broke his trance. He teetered through a rather generous number of gifts at the foot of the tree, the red and green and gold wrapping paper crinkling against his legs, before reaching the entryway, as he had many times before this one.

"Grandpa?" a child called from beyond the room, still unseen. A small girl bounced in, her bare feet smacking against the wooden floorboards. "Grandpa!" the girl shouted, running straight for him.

He knelt down to receive the bundle of arms and legs wrapping themselves around him.

"When did you get here?"

"Just a few moments ago. Where are your parents?"

The question filled his granddaughter with primal energy, excitement discharging through every nerve. She sped off deeper into the home to find them.

An eruption of voices followed as Nicholas and Emma entered, equally excited to see him as their daughter was.

Nicholas gave his father a hug, as did Emma, although it was a bit more awkward to make room for her pregnant belly.

"How are you feeling, young lady?"

"A little tired, especially with this one around," she said, pointing to her daughter, who was now hanging from her arm, climbing her like a tower.

"Will you be fine if I take this one for the night?" he said, putting his arm around Nicholas.

"I think so. I can't promise you I'll be in my right mind when you return, though."

Nicholas kissed Emma on the forehead.

"We'll be back before you know it."

"Dad! Can I come?"

Nicholas laughed. "Someday, but not today. Your grandfather and I have a lot of stops, but we can manage. We'll need your help soon enough. Just a while longer, Sam."

She pouted for a moment, but was soon distracted by the glint of bows and ribbons covering all manner of mystery under the Christmas tree.

"Where to first?" Nicholas asked his father.

"How about a little further than last time? Have you been to Canada?"

"Canada? Can't say I have."

"Nicholas, all those talents and you've barely left Scotland."

"There are plenty of children here who need gifts."

"Aye, plenty of children everywhere."

"Then it's good we have an infinite night ahead of us. Shall we begin?"

NICHOLAS and his father left his home and appeared on his Edinburgh rooftop. He looked down the lane towards the factory where his army turned craftsmen now lived and worked. It was a fine existence, a fine end to what could have been a tragedy for them. He wondered about how they fared outside of this place and the thought made him shudder.

"Are you ready?" his father asked.

He nodded.

"Something on your mind, son?"

"Are you going to tire of this? Coming here, seeing me, seeing them, wandering through this day of mine."

"I was robbed of a lifetime of this. I don't intend to let it end now, or ever, as long as you'll have me. Are you happy?"

"Most of the time. Sometimes when I look at her, I know it's not real, but then neither am I, and that makes it less of an illusion and more like something I can touch, if not hold. If you don't mind though, I think I'd like to keep this part just the two of us."

"I don't mind that at all."

Nicholas stared at a few brave stars chasing the fading light. He searched after constellations undiscovered, but found none. He craned his neck so that he saw nothing but the darkening night sky and he felt he was no longer under it, but flying above it, looking down at a sleeping world.

And so he was.

PREORDER BOOK TWO

**The Lunar Workshop Book 2:
She Cultivates Shadows**

What would you sacrifice for your family?
Time itself has been ruptured, and in the chaos of paradox beats the rapid heart of the next in line to take control of the Lunar Workshop—Emma Breugadaire's unborn child, a life that should no longer exist.

PREORDER ON AMAZON

RATE & REVIEW

I hope you enjoyed this book! I would be very grateful if you could spend just two or three minutes leaving a review (it can be as short as you like) on the book's Amazon store page or on Goodreads.

HISTORICAL NOTE

While The Lunar Workshop series is a work of historical fantasy, I do endeavour to represent the cultures, people, and events of the time as truthful and accurate. Writing about history is not a perfect science, and often the sources I discovered disagreed on minor points, but on the whole, I feel the period is represented well.

I spent three months in Edinburgh collecting research and primary sources to inform the layout, look, and feel of the city during the years of 1790 and 1810. While some of the characters in this novel do not conform to the expectations of the period, I wanted the environment and people around them to appear appropriately. Earlier drafts included dialect to ground the speech of every character to the time, but early readers found it too distracting. This was a change I feel was necessary for accessibility, but one that I made with reluctance.

I wish to identify two areas in which I deviated from history for convenience sake.

The first deviation occurs in the location of the story. Historically, the Luddites were mostly English textile workers and their movement started in Nottingham and spread throughout nearby regions. There is no record of the movement entering Scotland, which is why I treat the group of Luddites in this novel as an offshoot of the main rebellion. While this is a significant change, Scottish workers would have dealt with similar challenges as their occupations were industrialised and news of rebellions to the south would have reached them. In addition, the slight lag of the effects of industrialisation on Scotland created a more favourable timing for this particular story to be set there. Due to this, I made the decision to deviate on location, rather than the timing, of these events.

The second deviation doesn't have significant effects on the historicity of the novel, but I feel is important to note. The leader of the Luddites, Ned Ludd, was, by all accounts, not a real person. At most, the name was inspired by a well-known weaver, but even that is not confirmed. The fact that the leader of this movement was fabricated created an opportunity to fill that space with a character of my own, while remaining true to the fact that he was more a symbol than a real person. I will not spoil details here in case you are reading this before finishing the story, but I will say that the use of a man who watched the old ways of manufacturing be replaced by faster, less traditional approaches, while simultaneously experiencing the continued exploitation of child workers, was an opportunity befitting the mantle of the person my character eventually becomes.

I hope you will forgive any historical errors made in the service of telling this story, and I am happy to receive your thoughts and corrections as I continue to refine my research process and improve my adherence to history.

ACKNOWLEDGMENTS

Sonic the Hedgehog 3 released on February 2, 1994—Groundhog's Day. A lot of kids bought this video game. Several million, in fact. None of them got it as a gift for Christmas, though. After all, it was February.

That morning, my dad asked me and my brother to grab something from the storage closet in our basement. We shuffled down and pulled open the door. Inside, on top of a pile of dusty boxes, was Sonic the Hedgehog 3. There was a note included. I don't remember the exact words, but it was some sort of apology from an elf named Petrie. He explained that we were meant to get the game at Christmas, almost two months before anyone else in the world would play it, but that he had made a mistake and it wasn't delivered until that day.

You've probably already guessed that the game was purchased on release day and this little fiction was created to add to the fun of it all. That's not the point though. The point is that it was done at all. Christmas was particularly important to my dad and this character, Petrie the Elf, would become a recurring star over the years, popping up from time to time in all sorts of mischief. He could have just addressed the notes as the big guy himself, but he didn't. He went one step further, dug a little deeper, to create something to extend the wonder of his children by grounding the fiction.

This novel (and the two to follow) is a product of many people, but I don't think it would exist without my dad. It wasn't enough for me to write a story about this character. I had to dig deeper. I had to make it "real" by finding a historical origin to explain every loose end the accepted myths leave hanging.

I never breathed a word of this novel to my dad. It's as much a surprise to him as it is a love letter to the magic he created at Christmas. Thanks, Dad.

I also want to thank my first readers who took the plunge into a very messy second draft. Amy Dixon, my partner and love from page one to the very last period I will ever write. My brother, Cooper Bibaud, whose support is only second to the inspiration I pull from him. Kim Warner, who supports my work without reservation and one of the few people who's dared to tell me I'm wrong on multiple occasions. Leanne Stone, who was the first to hear the idea and who planted the seeds that would create a pull to Scotland that has never released.

I want to thank the Edinburgh Creative Writers Club for providing feedback on the opening chapters and not laughing me out of the room after hearing me read in a Scottish dialect. I still wake up in a cold sweat from time to time thinking about that. Oof. Additionally, I want to specifically thank Armarna Forbes, who gave me one small bit of advice I keep in the back of my mind always.

The biggest thanks to the Writers' Guild of Alberta for introducing me to Myrl Coulter, who had the largest impact on the final draft. A gifted author, a trusted editor, and someone who wasn't afraid to get into the weeds with me to find what makes this novel tick. I hope you're satisfied with the result.

I had a few editors over the years look at different elements. Sarah Robins, who, after reading a sex scene, simply wrote, "Do people like this?" I immediately rewrote it.

Also, thank you to Hailey Peterson for her final review of my story. Your polish and recommendations were the final touch I needed to feel good about locking in the final draft.

It's always so striking to me that at the end of something that feels so lonesome in its creation, was, in fact, infused with dozens of voices.

Before I end, I owe a great deal to the cafes who let me sit at their tables for hours on end, sometimes with only a cup of tea to show for it.

Here, in no particular order, is the list of cafes I wrote this story in.

- The Tea Girl | Edmonton, Canada
- Art of Cake | Edmonton, Canada
- Deville Cafe | Edmonton, Canada
- Lock Stock | Edmonton, Canada
- The Colombian | Edmonton, Canada
- Credo Cafe | Edmonton, Canada
- Remedy | Edmonton, Canada
- Transcend Coffee | Edmonton, Canada
- Block 1912 | Edmonton, Canada
- Little Brick | Edmonton, Canada
- District Cafe & Bakery | Edmonton, Canada
- DOSC | Edmonton, Canada
- Iconoclast Coffee Roasters | Edmonton, Canada
- Cafe Versailles | Edmonton, Canada
- Mandolin Books and Coffee Co. | Edmonton, Canada
- Blendz | Edmonton, Canada
- Second Cup, Oliver | Edmonton, Canada
- Starbucks, Brewery District | Edmonton, Canada
- Café Medina | Vancouver, Canada
- Restaurant Evangeline | Chéticamp, Canada
- Kaph | Dublin, Ireland
- Café Marlayne | Edinburgh, Scotland
- Black Medicine Coffee Co | Edinburgh, Scotland
- Café Renroc | Edinburgh, Scotland
- The Foot of the Walk | Edinburgh, Scotland
- The Lioness of Leith | Edinburgh, Scotland

- Starbucks, Leith Walk | Edinburgh, Scotland
- Shakespeare and Sons | Berlin, Germany
- leuchtstoff - Kaffeebar und Bakery | Berlin, Germany
- Café Katulki | Berlin, Germany
- Kawiarnia Literacka | Kraków, Poland
- Brolenda Coffee Shop | Toulouse, France
- Starbucks | Toulouse, France
- Bar restaurante El Rincón de la Huerta | Seville, Spain
- Café Tarifa | Seville, Spain
- Forza Cafe | Kotor, Montenegro
- Old Winery Wine Bar | Kotor, Montenegro
- Ala Mizerija | Dubrovnik, Croatia
- Magvető Café | Budapest, Hungary
- Kelet Kávézó és Galéria | Budapest, Hungary
- Madal Cafe | Budapest, Hungary
- Rengeteg RomKafé | Budapest, Hungary
- MOC Bomonti | Istanbul, Turkey

Get your FREE ebook!

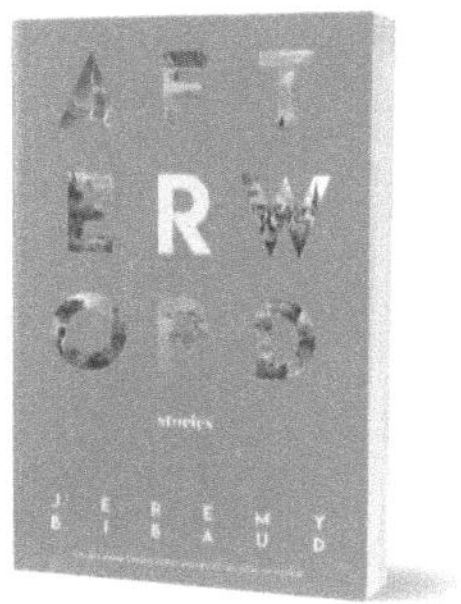

Thanks for supporting my work.
As a small token, I want to send you a gift!

Afterword is a collection of 12 pieces of short historical fiction based on the weirdest and wildest jobs that no longer exist.

You can get your free ebook by scanning the code below or visiting my website at jeremybibaud.com

ABOUT THE AUTHOR

Jeremy Bibaud is a Canadian writer living in Edmonton, Alberta, and editor of the award-winning *Funicular Magazine,* which publishes short fiction and poetry. His fiction most recently won *F(r)iction*'s Summer Literary Contest, judged by Nebula and Locus Award winner Alyssa Wong. His stories have been found on thousands of coffee cups, in Canada's first short story machine, and in publications like *FreeFall, F(r)iction, Short Edition, YEGWords, Burning Water,* and *Dactyl.*

His first publication, *Afterword,* a collection of 12 pieces of historical fiction, is available now.

www.ingramcontent.com/pod-product-compliance
Lightning Source LLC
Chambersburg PA
CBHW030535310726
48979CB00010B/1921/J
9781778135651